paper teeth

PAPER

TEETH

Lauralyn Chow

NeWest Press

Library and Archives Canada Cataloguing in Publication

Chow, Lauralyn, author
Paper teeth / Lauralyn Chow.

(Nunatak first fiction series ; no. 43)
Short stories.
Issued in print and electronic formats.
ISBN 978-1-926455-63-1 (paperback).
ISBN 978-1-926455-64-8 (epub).
ISBN 978-1-926455-65-5 (mobi)

I. Title. II. Series: Nunatak first fiction ; no. 43

PS8605.H7P37 2016   C813'.6   C2016-901682-X   C2016-901683-8

Editor: Nicole Markotić
Book design: Natalie Olsen, Kisscut Design
Author photo: The Estate of Sam Chow

Paper Teeth is a work of fiction. Names, characters, places, incidents and dialogue, and all characters with the exception of some well-known historical and public figures, are products of the author's imagination or are used fictitiously. Where actual institutions and real-life historical figures appear, the situations, incidents and dialogues concerning those entities and persons are entirely fictional and are not intended to describe actual events. In all other respects, any resemblance to actual events, locales, or persons, living or dead, is entirely coincidental.

    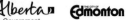

NeWest Press acknowledges the support of the Canada Council for the Arts, the Alberta Foundation for the Arts, and the Edmonton Arts Council for support of our publishing program. This project is funded in part by the Government of Canada.

 # 201, 8540 – 109 Street
Edmonton, Alberta T6G 1E6
780.432.9427
NeWest Press www.newestpress.com

No bison were harmed in the making of this book.
Printed and bound in Canada
1 2 3 4 5   18 17 16

In memory of my parents,
Sam and Mary Chow

Preface

Chrome paper napkin dispensers, mini-juke boxes at each Formica tabletop booth, a tall paper calendar on the wall at the back featuring a Chinese ink drawing of a pink orchid in a square plant pot, an illuminated analogue wall clock with rectangular flip-down advertising, a small plastic cog flipping the plastic pages of the ads down every fifteen seconds, (Silverwood's Dairy, Player's Navy Cut Cigarettes - Filter, Texaco Motor Oils, Allstate Insurance), a jade plant, round white tea pots filled with leaves and boiling water.

Round banquet tables, covered with white cotton tablecloths, in turn covered by large round Lazy Susans, enormous rectangular fish tanks (lyretail mollies, angel fish, neon tetras, bronze catfish, orange swordtails, bleeding heart tetras, kissing gouramis) with aerators disguised as plastic deep sea divers, illuminated cigarette vending machines with chrome-plated pull knobs, behind the host's desk, a large glass mirror etched with sprays of leaves and flowers.

Small red-and-gold altars, incense spiraling smoke, golden statues, tiny vertical banners of Chinese calligraphy, oranges.

A multi-page English language menu (sometimes bilingual with Chinese writing), plastic laminated, offering forty-seven, eighty-eight, one hundred and twenty-nine, different Chinese dishes, all listed by number. Sometimes, one printed page in the menu for Western cuisine. At the back of the menu, a short list of beverages. No pots of Chinese tea or bowls of steamed rice; these come to the table under their own steam.

A Chinese language menu (never bilingual), written on pink paper, sometimes in a plastic pocket inside the English menu, sometimes in a plastic page protector given only to certain guests, listing at most seven dishes.

An unwritten menu of non-replicable Chinese dishes, food that no other table is served, after Dad goes into the kitchen, only with his son, to visit with his friends, the cooks.

Of course, you are bilingual, English and French (un petit peu). No Chinese, though. In Chinese restaurants, you only eat un-scripted, Chinese food from the unwritten menu for the first half of your life. The calendar flips. On your family tree, you get closer and closer to the ground. On your family tree, no one eats from the unwritten menu anymore.

Illiteracy makes you hungry.

PAPER
TEETH

Today's Menu

....

Number 25. Eight Precious Jewels with Bean Cake

"Please, Dad?"

Right beneath his chest bone, Dad feels six day's worth of gravity pinning him to the driver's seat. Gravity from feeding the big dreams that Mumma dreams for everyone: herself, Dad, the kids, extended family, neighbours, the world. Gravity in knowing that winning bread makes life a game, a competition with real stakes and not a small amount left to chance. Gravity in discerning that the playing field has nothing to do with play.

Dad thanks the Lord for his plead-y, needy kids, because sometimes, on the seventh day, Dad gets to flay gravity wide open to a place with no game-playing, no stakes, no worries. Dad seesaws on his sit bones. He scans the smooth asphalt ribbon before him, then the rearview mirror, and finds three pairs of hopeful, supplicating eyes.

....

"Airplane ride?"

"Yeah, Dad, Please?"

The youngest, Jane, sits quietly in the front seat between him and Mumma, her lips resembling a thin curved darning needle, both ends pointing down. She stares at the radio dials, her eyebrows connected by ragged worry lines, premature wrinkles for any preschooler. Dad senses that for Jane, there's never a seventh day.

"Ah please, Dad?" Tom, his only son, begs one more time.

The sound of an engine suddenly submitting to a command to speed and the palpable acceleration captures the attention of every passenger. As they approach the House of the Lord, the white Pontiac Strato-Chief attains peak velocity at the crest of the hill, and soars over the 109th Street overpass, locally known as the Rat Hole, leaving six days of Gravity to eat dust. No one hears the metallic springs and shocks of the car's suspension banging and resettling the chassis. Not for all the giggling and hooting and cheering, all enlivened by the disbelief that yet again, Dad, the very model of seriousness and sobriety, caution and responsibility, just did something illegal, a little bit dangerous, and so much fun. Squeeee! After a week of being so good, what a thrill (for most of them) to be capital N naughty. After all the commotion has died down, what a fly inside the car might hear is Mumma's stiletto heel being withdrawn from the new hole punched in the rubber floor mat, a round hole just below where the brake pedal might be if the front passenger's side of the Strato-Chief's bench seat came with a brake.

Sandwiched between the bread of the Foon Kee Bean Cake Company and the Coffee Cup Inn stands the House of the Lord. The Coffee Cup Inn, a whitewashed building in the shape of a giant coffee cup, pessimistically surveys the street through grimy, hexagonal-shaped windows. Two brown stripes near the flat roof line mimic the heavy whiteware cups used to serve up, or so the big sign says, Hot Coffee, Best Cup in Town. Another sign hangs in the top window pane of the aluminum screen door, says Closed. The building slumps over most of the lot that it sits on, the big coffee cup threatening to tip over and spill on its crumbling asphalt saucer. A narrow sidewalk with big cracks rounds the little corner lot.

The Foon Kee Bean Cake Company occupies a grey stucco saltbox house, three skinny wood-framed windows bunch together at the front, with three round ventilation holes at the bottom of each window. Someone's planted a painted sign on two wooden stakes at an angle to the sidewalk. Red letters advertise: "Foon Kee Bean Cake Company," and then Chinese calligraphy which says God knows what. Shards of white paint have peeled away from both the sign and the window frames, the exposed wood weathered silvery grey. No one in the Lee family ever sees anyone inside the house, or coming out with a nicely tied bundle of funky bean cake. That's the kids' joke: Foon kee bean cake, What's that foon kee smell?, P-U, must be that foon kee bean cake. Mumma doesn't buy her tofu there. Mumma's bean cake isn't funky, although it may be foon kee, God knows.

On Communion Sundays only, the Lees park the car across the avenue from the Coffee Cup Inn behind a brick flatiron building, the House of the Lord does not offer ample parking. On the Jasper Avenue side of the flatiron building, over one of three wooden doors without numbers, a solitary blue sign in the shape of a long sideways capsule hangs, with white letters which read "Turkish Baths." Above the lettering, the sign painter has created a painting of a woman, with orange Gibson Girl hair. A woman taking a bath. She's lowered herself into the blue sign, her back to the street, her undrawn parts engaged in the pleasure of Turkish Baths. Her head in profile shows a long comma of a nostril, turned slightly upward, the alabaster skin on her back faded by the sun. Bits of plywood show through parts of her skin, but a black curvy line running the length of her back is continuous. Even on Sunday, pink neon lines pelt her about the shoulders, and the same colour bubbles froth on and off, concentrating at her waist and parts below.

The parking space behind the flatiron building is best for the fast getaway onto Jasper Avenue, and for giving the kids a look at the woman taking a bath: Lizzie, the oldest, wonders what makes a bath a Turkish bath, is it the tub or the bubbles, do they put something in the water, is it deep like a swimming pool or shallow like the fish hatchery; Pen, her sister, has warm panty thoughts, she's bathing nude on Jasper Avenue where everyone çan see her; Tom lets his eyes follow the sign as it flows past the car side window, wishes you didn't have to be from Turkey to go in there; Jane frowns, why does she always have to sit on the hump, one saddle shoe resting on either side of the carpeted hump on the car floor? On every fast getaway onto Jasper Avenue, Mumma looks at the bather in Turkish Baths and wraps the front selvages of her coat, one in each hand, a little closer around her body, arms crossed, balled fists hiding behind her elbows.

Mumma sees him first. One Communion Sunday, as the Lee family walks single file, as Dad, then Lizzie, Pen, Tom, Jane and Mumma walk on the narrow broken sidewalk around the Coffee Cup Inn on the way to the House of the Lord, Mumma sees him first.

"Look," says Pen, "I see someone's bum-bum. See? Uh-ohh, London France no underpants. See the top of his cra —"

"Pen, don't point. Shhhh," Mumma hisses from the back of the line. "He's sleeping. Everybody, keep moving. C'mon Dad, keep moving."

There's no one else around. One of the man's tan-coloured boots stands upright on the asphalt at the side of the building, near the handle. The boot gapes open, the lace threaded loosely through the bottom holes, the tongue pulled all the way down.

His feet barely touch the ground. Bent from the waist, the man lies face down through the handle of the Coffee Cup Inn, one boot on and one boot off, as if, in an attempt to dive through the handle, he only made it half way through and fell asleep.

As if. That's one way to describe what the Lee family sees, one version. As if the man carefully took one boot off, to keep it nice, just in case, as he considered the puzzler of how to dive through the handle of the big coffee cup. As if he attempted to permute the trajectory calculations, velocity, point of departure, angle of projectile. As if the man, only a fair student in Grade 10 Physics, had made a life-defining decision to take Algebra instead of Physics 20, so that years later, outside the Coffee

Cup Inn, at the moment of recall, a glass of water spilled on his mental notes concerning velocity, rendering them illegible. As if narcolepsy travelled up and down the man's family tree like an irrepressible monkey on speed, hitting the man's Uncle Billy hard. As if Billy, so the story goes, one day drove fifteen miles, took a cup of tea and toast with his brother Al, drove the fifteen miles home, all in his sleep, and does not remember a thing. As if narcolepsy almost missed Billy's nephew, but a split second after he sprang into the air, narcolepsy grabbed him by the round knobs of his ankle bones, easier because of the preceding boot removal, and pulled him down to sleep in the cradle of a building handle. As if all that is how the Lee family comes to see the sleeping man and his bum, hanging by his waist through the handle of the Coffee Cup Inn on Communion Sunday. As if.

During that Communion, Mumma purses her lips into a small kiss to drink her tiny glass of Welch's grape juice. As she bends her head to pray, she thinks, what if the man managed to get himself down from the handle, what if he staggered around and walked towards them, followed them here to the House of the Lord. What then? When Tom dips his fingers into the almost empty glass that Mumma has just returned to the wooden cup holder in front of them, she doesn't quietly smack his hand and return it to his lap. Tom's mouth gapes at Mumma who has her eyes closed, her head bent. He wipes the juicy-damp fingers on his corduroy pants and benches his own hands to his lap.

....

One night during the week before the next Communion Sunday, Mumma and Dad's post-prandial conversation at the dinner table becomes budget dinner theatre for the kids — no dessert bar, but what a show. While the Anglophone kids would benefit from English subtitles providing instantaneous translation, that service will never be provided. The kids are not the intended audience, but they enjoy the body language, moving their heads back and forth to whoever speaks. Tonight's drama is replete with body English, the food and table buried by windshield wiper hands arcing through the air, and forehead lines that magically appear like a Roman window blind drawn open by suddenly wide open eyes. In tonight's drama, one character, Mystery Language, is a charismatic magnet, her monologue in two voices hidden in plain hearing.

Lizzie thinks her parents are discussing Communion this Sunday, Lizzie hears "Gawfeah Gup Ian" when Mumma talks. Tom thinks Dad is trying to explain to Mumma a possible loophole that will get Tom into Turkish Baths, hears Dad say "Gajasper Avanue." Jane is the only one dead certain of her ability to interpret Chinese, at least some of the words. "Bei" [*the verb, to give*] means Big, "Douw" [*the verb, to touch*] means Doll, and "Wah Nynh" [*the Chinese name of a family friend the kids call Uncle Freddy*] means Walking; her birthday is only five months away but Jane knows Mumma is going to buy her a real, live walking doll. They must not agree on which doll to buy, because they're talking, talking, talking, Jane thinks, but this is a big, important decision, so lots of talking makes sense. Jane hopes they settle on Little Francine and not Betsy Bell, because Little Francine has a green velvet coat, with a real fur collar and she also comes with a heart-shaped locket that Jane could wear. To make sure they pick Little Francine, Jane knows she has to be careful how she brings this up with Mumma, Gimmee-Gimmees Never Get, but not too careful because Mumma can be so wrong about important things. [Note: Years from now, when there is colour television, Mumma's children will watch l'Hockey on the Canadian French language network whenever there is a game blackout for the local station, because their understanding of the language is not critical to enjoying the game.] Pen doesn't care what they're talking about. Although she has finished eating, Pen holds a sliver of beef between her chopsticks, pressing the morsel against the side of a small plate beside her rice bowl, until as much of the garlic and black bean sauce as possible runs out in a brown, aromatic rivulet.

....

"What did you say to them, Mumma?" Lizzie leans against Mumma's coat, and whispers. The women in the House of the Lord cheerily endure the Lee children's reserved manner once every month when the Lee family comes for Communion Sunday, swarming the Lee family pew, one of the eight pews donated by Dad. They will retreat, just as the choir processes down the centre aisle. Before that, in Chinese, they chatter excitedly, non-stop, every one, simultaneously, One Body with many mouths and multiple animated hands. They pinch Tom's cheeks, move the skin all around his cheekbones. They take hold of the girls' white-gloved hands, by the palms, to display the even stitching to each other, the posies of embroidered flowers on the backs of the girls' gloved hands. While being gentle with their gloved hands, the women pinch and finger the nap of the girls' coat sleeves, navy in Winter, beige in Spring. They never finger anything but the garments, never pinch or touch the girls' arms.

As Mumma settles her purse on the floor, and opens her Order of Service, she replies, "I told them that your first language, of course, is Chinese, like I always tell them, but that you're all a little shy." Mumma says, shy, like shyness is in the same family of character traits as being vain, feckless, snooty. Mumma's quiet voice sounds breathy but no more quiet than her normal speaking voice.

"That's not true." Sitting beside her in the pew, Lizzie turns to Mumma so Mumma can't miss her peevish frown.

"Sure. I spoke Chinese to all of you when you were babies."

"Mumma, we don't speak Chinese. Period. And we're not shy," Lizzie whispers.

"I didn't tell them you spoke Chinese. And if you're not shy, why don't you sing in the choir, that's what they want to know."

"Because we don't speak Chinese, or sing Chinese. And, no one in the choir sings English." Lizzie's whispered words come out faster and faster.

"You could go to Chinese school, like I did. You could go to school for three hours a day, after regular school, just like I did."

"Where?"

"I could find a school. You should sing in the choir, you have a lovely voice."

Mumma takes one of the Chinese Bibles from the stand attached to the back of the pew facing her, opens it, and pretends to follow the scripture reading. With all her Chinese schooling, the kids know Mumma still doesn't read Chinese.

Lizzie's eyes roll clockwise, her mouth curls downward at one corner, a rhetorical question mark lying on its side. She's not shy, but she doesn't know what to say. Both Mumma and Dad's eyebrows tell her she better not say, I don't speak Chinese, or read it, or understand it. She shakes her head, opens the Bible she brings from home to where the *Miss Chatelaine* article on "Healthy, Glowing Skin and How to Get It" lies, each page carefully cut in quarters to fit the pages. Lizzie used to look up at the Minister, Reverend Fahn See (to the English-speaking world, "Jerry") Muon, once in a while, pretended to comprehend, to follow along in her Bible, but the minister lobbed ball after ball to absolutely everyone else he faced and not her, so Lizzie, an avid tennis player, felt her gesture an unnecessary net ball interfering with a game in progress.

Tom rubs his red cheeks with both hands, his feet swing back and forth. He already has folded one Order of Service paper airplane, and if he hadn't kicked Jane and got the pencil taken away, they could have played Hangman, even though he's a terrible speller and she can't read.

The game started out all right, "You wanna play Hangman, Jane?"

"No."

"Yeah. Let's play Hangman."

"No. I don't want to."

"OK, I'll go first. Here," he said, handing her his Order of Service, with seven pencilled dashes at the empty space near the bottom, and a line drawing of a gallows.

"I'm not plaaaying," Jane pushed the Order of Service back into Tom's hand.

"Oh, so you guess, 'A'. Nope, no 'A'. That's your head." He drew a round circle under the gallows with a short pencil wedged into the wooden holder for offering envelopes.

"Stop it. I'm not playing."

"Right, now you're guessing, 'P'. Yeah, there's one 'P'."

"I said I'm not playing. Stop, Tom."

"Make me."

"I haven't got the recipe — Mumma!"

Now Jane's sitting beside Lizzie, and Pen will give his arm rope burn if he bugs her, so no Hangman today. Too bad. Tom pokes Dad's arm and opens the front of his little black blazer, pointing to the inside towards his heart. Dad reaches into his suit jacket and, clicking it down, passes Tom a black ballpoint pen. Tom draws a stick figure hanging from a noose with almond-shaped eyes, and little braids, just like Jane's. He shows Jane the picture, then pantomimes her demise, his hands around his neck, choke choke choke, eyes rolled back, tongue out, head bobbing. Dad slides the pen out of Tom's hand, clicks it shut and pockets the pen. He takes the airplane with the Chinese girl effigy out of the Bible rack, where Tom has stuffed it, and puts it in Tom's hand. Tom thinks, dim sum after church. Yum. At least there's dim sum after a whole hour of this. Char siu bao, har gow, siu mai, pai gwut. Didn't get him very far in Sunday School the last time he went, but it's the only Chinese he knows. Tom bends forward from the waist and considers his dad's profile, Dad who can read, write and talk Chinese. Dad's good at fake paying attention, Tom thinks. Just a sec now, looks like Dad's actually paying attention. Holy cow and a calf. Tom shakes his head, whatever bangs your bongos, as Pen would say. Barbeque pork buns, maids' caps, shrimp balls, black bean spare ribs. Mmmm. Tom reaches over to turn Dad's wrist towards him. Only one big notch after the 12 and the little hand still on the notch before, Tom inhales one deep breath. Both hands have to be on 12 for dim sum. Tom fingers the small plastic wings keeping his comes-already-tied tie under his shirt collar. The air blows out of Tom's rounded lips. Oh, Tom shuffles to his feet as everyone else stands. They must be singing a hymn. Why does Church take a hundred times longer than an hour of cartoons?

Pen flips quickly through her fashion pictures in the centre of her Bible that she, too, brings from home. Thirteen now, she'll never have a *Seventeen* magazine that isn't cut to pieces. Sometimes, she has to cut one picture in half, to fit inside the pages. The pants, shoes and the body of a handbag captured in one clipping, and the crocheted top, hair, makeup and jewellery in the next. She studies the magazine photos without even noticing the caption, "It's All About Hue." Pen needs less than five minutes to prep a *Seventeen*, *Glamour*, or *Ingenue* for church, flipping with her ring and baby fingers past the articles to the next segment of photos, the rest of her hand holding impatient scissors. Pen isn't interested in reading in church or anywhere else for that matter. Her knowledge of fashion design and colour, of *Glamour* Do's and Don'ts came factory installed, no operator's manual required. Pen plans an ideal wardrobe for hours every day, but once a month, at church, the drawings, the fabric swatches, and colour details have to be sketched into her book later, in her bedroom. Pen does some of her best design work in church, who knows what magic the reverend weaves, maybe good old Muon-go Jerry creates a mood. For that, she bears the monthly gauntlet of church ladies in and out of the building. But today, a stingy, scrubby miasma substitutes for the expansive creative spirit, which ticks off Pen. In the same way Mr. Clarke, her social studies teacher, annoys her by messing up the emphasis in words, putting stress on the wrong syllable, Pen feels her patience barometer dropping very low. Pen can see Mr. Clarke in her mind, bracketed at his wooden desk by pillars of his beloved *National Geographic* magazines. When they study Italy, he talks about NeapoLItan society, you all know NeapoLItan ice cream, he says, pushing the centre of his glasses higher on his nose. Stupid Clarke, Pen thinks, always has his emPHAsis messed up. This week, God, the AboriGEANIES of Australia. Pen feels for the Aborigines, teachers like Clarke pretending to know all about them, fingering their pictures in the pages of *National Geographic*, giving them names like AboriGEANIES. Pen picks a piece of lint off her coat sleeve, why is she even thinking about Mr. Clarke at church when she should be pairing coal-coloured knee socks with blanket plaid skirts?

Jane sits still, fixed on the minister's mouth. Mumma has read to her the typewritten English words on the Order of Service, "Chinese United Church," and the street address, but the rest of the page only has some numbers, and handwritten Chinese calligraphy. Doesn't matter, Jane understands Chinese, even if she can't read.

"Mumma, what is 'Yeah, Sookey Duke'," Jane asks Mumma one day.

"What?"

"What's 'Yeah, Sookey Duke'?"

"Who says that?"

"At church. The minister says it over and over and over."

"Yeay soh gay dew?"

"Yeah, Sookey Duke!"

"The House of the Lord. Yeay soh gay dew."

"Oh, so every time he says that, that's what he means?"

"Mm-hmm."

The House of the Lord. Big walking dolly. Jane taps her fingers on either side of the pew beside her legs, and then she starts to nod her head from side to side, until momentum quickly has her whole body rocking on her sit bones, toes tapping, just waiting for the minister to say Yeay soh gay dew. He's been talking a very, very long time, until, Whooap! Jane's little white-gloved fingers leap up in front of her animated face. "House of the Lord," she whispers quickly, then lowers her fingers to stroke the top of the pew in front of her.

That House of the Lord stuff, she figured out a few Communion Sundays ago, and other than walking dolly, no other words since. At this rate, how can you learn all the Chinese words in just one lifetime, she wonders. Jane feels the pretend weight of sand on her eyelids, and turns Lizzie's wrist towards her. Big hand only on number 3. No no, only number 3? Jane wags a gloved pointer finger at Lizzie's naughty watch. About a year ago, Jane started to pretend to fall asleep, have a little nap, after things started rolling, and then she just started to fall asleep, ha, so she didn't have to go downstairs with Tom and all the other kids to Sunday School. There's not many kids, but all of them speak Chinese, and really fast, and they give her neh-neh-Neh-neh-neh looks because she doesn't get it when the Sunday School teacher talks, or at least not as fast as the other kids. It's not fair, because she's good at playschool, but not Sunday School. And the kids don't bug Tom, even though he doesn't speak Chinese either. As Jane's eyes close, she wonders why some ladies wear their pyjamas and slippers to church, they must get up even later than Jane. "House of the Lord," she whispers, as her white gloves flash beside her closed eyes. Jane's sleep breathing as she dreamwishes that she wakes up in time for Communion, please, because she's only seen it a few times. When Mumma has coffee with Mrs. Walker in the kitchen, Jane sneaks tiny pastel Tupperware containers, the ones that hold only one extra egg yolk, into the living room, and she does Communion with her dollies, using water from the bathroom and buttered egg loaf bread she tears into tiny pieces.

"Why don't you use your tea set to play with your dollies?" Mumma asks.

As if a tea set would work. As if.

....

"I ate too much; I think I'm going to be sick," Tom says. Every time, Tom eats too much and says he's going to be sick as they're walking back to the car, single file. Tom never gets sick, at least never after dim sum on Communion Sundays. [Note: The potential to learn from their personal childhood experiences gets completely overrun by Tom's incessant post-dim sum lament, his gastro-version of *The Boy Who Cried Wolf*. And thus, when they have their own children, Tom and his sisters will find out the messy way that, unlike Tom after eating too much dim sum, their children, like the vast majority of kids who say they're going to be sick, are uncannily prophetic.]

25

"Don't eat so much, Father Brady says gluttony's a sin," Dad responds, every time, and then, apropos to nothing, he says, "That was good service." No one in the Lee family ever knows whether Dad says, "a good service" or, "uh, good service," whether he means a good Communion Sunday worship service, or, good service from Doug, the waiter at the New World Restaurant. No one ever asks. Although they come only once a month, Doug brings the first large china platter of steamed shrimp maids' caps to the table as the Lee family settles into their booth in the New World. From the window of the New World, Doug watches Ah Bahk and his family come out of the church from across the street and jaywalk to dim sum, little hand on the 12, big hand sliding from the first notch. Doug walks briskly to the kitchen. He had spotted Dad's car on the street when he arrived at the restaurant this morning, and set the table for six: six pairs of chopsticks, six tea cups and six small white plates, and six white porcelain soup spoons. When the bell rang at St. Barbara's up the street, Doug took his place at his window to time the first plate exactly.

Some families having dim sum order off a menu, but Doug knows the Lee family's choices never change. Doug flicks his wrist, and everyone watches the white damask napkins, one after the other, spin like a full skirt with deep gores on the tip of his finger. He safely lands one whirling napkin on each of their laps, then brings a big white teapot filled with green tea. Doug talks to Dad and pretends not to watch Mumma wipe out all the Chinese tea cups with a paper napkin from the chrome dispenser on the table. Doug fills each tea cup, and places one in front of every member of the family, saying their family positions in Chinese: respected uncle, respected aunt, eldest daughter, daughter number two, little brother, baby sister. [Note: In the 1970s, when the New World reconstitutes as the Old Cathayan, and then again, with a big catty-corner hop down the street, as The Jumbo, dim sum will evolve into a melee of young women shouting out the names of additive-laden dishes, "there is little bit of MSG," they will shout, reeling those dishes in institutional metal carts around crowded tables, and God help you if you are seated at the last table to be served near the swinging doors at the back. When dim sum will become like grocery shopping behind the looking glass, where people will sit still and eat off carts of food flying by, Doug will become a successful Assistant Cook II in a hospital kitchen and will never have the time, space or inclination inside the kitchen to spin napkins, let alone listen for the bells at St. Barb's.]

....

Outside the New World, the sun glares off the sidewalk, and Jane and Lizzie use their hands as visors to shade their eyes. Everyone looks both ways, then the Lee family jaywalks back across the street in a clump. The single file line re-forms on the narrow sidewalk in front of the church.

"Hey," Pen starts, "let's go buy some foon kee bean cake. Go ring the bell, Tom."

"No."

"Go ring it. I dare you. Mmm, foon kee bean cake."

"I ate too much; I think I'm going to be sick."

"Don't eat so much, Father Brady says gluttony's a sin," says Dad, "That was good service."

"We're going the wrong way," Jane says from the back, as they cross the avenue, "Hey, we're going the wrong way."

"No, we're not," says Pen.

"No, we're not," Tom says, turning around, he tucks a middle finger behind his thumb in a circle, flicks Jane in the forehead, "Dummy."

"Owww."

"Stop flicking your sister," Mumma says.

Two boarded doors down from the Foon Kee Bean Cake Company, and across the road, a long, low one-storey building with baby blue wood siding squats, still recovering, by all appearances, from being slammed down, hard, on the lot. Wrapped inside the baby blue siding, a pawn shop sits on the corner. The sidewalk invites a limitless number of mothers' broken backs, cement half-blocks, frost heaved and cracked into a dusty grey mosaic. The single file line bumps and rolls as arms reach out for balance, feet take on the multiple slopes of the broken path.

On the flat roof of the pawn shop, right over the doorway, a big brown bear stands on its back legs, stuffed and mounted, and secured to the roof by four guy-wires. [Note: It will be years before any of the Lee children befriend (then betroth, then beget, hmmm, so many other stories) some naughty biologists who regale the whole family with all the rules for sexing animals, so, with this taxidermied specimen missing obvious markers, think of the bear as Guy, male, only because of the wires keeping him up or possibly holding him down.] Standing, his mouth open, front paws reaching out, the bear does not elicit fear, pity, or reverence for nature, being none of ferocious, pathetic or majestic, but gives the feeling that he is calling out, "Hey. Hello. Hello? Anybody? Hello."

As the single file procession rounds the corner, moves beyond the bear's peripheral vision, the Lee family car comes into view. But the line stops before reaching the car, underneath a high open window at the side of the pawn shop with a thick blue wire screen.

"They're still at it," Pen whispers.

"Shhh," Mumma whispers, "get away from that window."

Jane's confusion brings out her forehead worry lines, her mouth a very curved darning needle. Same thing happened on the way to church, that same sound. Jane thought she recognized the sound coming from the window as mah jong tiles being swirled in a circle, then stacked up into long walls like the dads do at house parties. But this was daytime, not nighttime, and where was the *Hockey Night in Canada* sound from the television, blaring beside the tables set up to play mah jong? And the talk talk talk, and laughing sounds that the dads make, sitting on folding chairs around the square card tables, smoking, long mah jong tile walls in front of each dad. Where's that sound? And what about the sound of the bossa nova records Auntie Vee brings for the mummas listen to, bossa nova, while they dance a little bit in front of the stereo console, munch on homemade Poppycock, and talk about what Margot Oliver is cooking in *Weekend* magazine? What about the sparkly sounds of the mummas talking, flipping magazine pages, and listening to bossa nova records? No people sounds, no party sounds coming out of the window by the bear, no, can't be a house party, so, Jane concludes, can't be mah jong I'm hearing. Sure sounds like mah jong, but in a flash of insight, Jane grasps that the window right there beside the pawn shop is a main floor window, not a basement one, not a window to a rumpus room where the children run down the stairs to stand beside their dads and watch them play, and then, when they're booted out for making too much noise, come back upstairs to sit quietly with Auntie Vee and the mummas for a moment, begging for bits of sugary popcorn and feigning interest in the stacks of handwritten recipe cards on the coffee table. So, ha, cannot be mah jong she's hearing.

Tom jumps for a better view, and Mumma swats him on the arm as he lands.

"Are they still playing?" Pen asks.

"Yup, four guys still playing," Tom replies.

"Shhhhh," Mumma whispers.

"Who's playing?" Jane asks loudly, "Playing what?"

"Shhhh," Mumma whispers a little louder.

"Mah jong," Tom says, "four men playing Mah —"

Mumma grabs Tom by the arm and pulls him towards the car, "Did you hear me?"

"Anyone we know?" Pen asks Tom as they pile into the backseat.

"No," Dad says, last one in the car, closing the driver's door behind him as the final punctuation to this subject, "No one you know."

The sound of mah jong tiles swirling in a circle continues to flow out the window beside the pawn shop, the flow controlled by four anonymous players. Eight unseen hands wash the tiles, funnelling and impelling. Funnelling and impelling the smooth lacquered tablets, four players create a man-made tile whirlpool. And Mumma's children identify the sounds of the unseen cycle, of tiles being stacked, collected and discarded, included, excluded.

And when the Lee family gets home, Dad will take out his mah jong set and teach Mumma's children all the moves, the washing of the tiles, moving and stacking them into bars like refrigerator cookie dough.

And the children will feel the thrill of washing the tiles, all one hundred forty-four tiles making their way towards each child in a moving mass, while all the players simultaneously amass and then push all the tiles away from themselves, leaving each person with the transcendent feeling of possessing everything and nothing all at once.

"See, there are nine balls, nine bamboo, nine characters — see the characters, those are the numbers in Chinese, and the symbol for each number is a simple line drawing of that number," Dad says, "One to nine. Easy."

"No they're not," Pen says, inverting the seven tile face down and up between her thumb and forefinger, "That doesn't even make sense."

"Yes, those pictures are ideograms," Dad says, "Look, every symbol is a little picture of every single number, one is one line, two is two lines, three —"

"Ooo, these are pretty, they look like flowers," Jane says, cupping her hands around eight tiles that Dad has separated out into a line.

"They are flowers," Dad replies enthusiastically, "But no, Little One, not those ones, those are the seasons."

Jane bares her curved darning needle pout, "No. They're all flowers. They look like flowers. They're flowers."

Dad tries another tack. "Son, do you see the winds?" Dad asks Tom, bracing four tiles between his fingers.

Skepticism widens Tom's eyes. His Boy Scout shoes have a real compass in the heel, covered by a round leather patch, and Tom's already learned about things like NNW.

"Dad, there's way more than four wind directions, there's, I dunno, like, sixteen. This is primitive, way too old timey. And how can you tell those tiles apart anyway?"

Dad resists the teachable moment, the temptation to inform his son that in ancient China, mariners used a 24-point compass that did not fit in the heel of a Boy Scout shoe. Instead, he says, "The game has lasted a long time, but that doesn't make mah jong primitive. To answer your question, you tell the wind tiles apart by learning to tell them apart, period. Are any of you interested in learning the basic strategy?"

"I guess," Tom says.

"Sure," Lizzie shrugs her shoulders, "why not?"

"Whatever." Pen's tongue explores the inside of her flaccid mouth.

"I like the flowers," Jane says, stroking the faces of the eight flower and season tiles.

Dad is an excellent mah jong player, and a great teacher, he's taught most of them how to play tennis, so how hard can this be, he thinks.

Ball after ball, Dad will gently lob balls from the game of mah jong perfectly into their court, all the rules, the tile properties, basic strategy, how to win. And even though both Lizzie and Tom will be holders of provincial tennis titles, and Pen a runner-up and Jane a somewhat proficient ball girl at the community tennis courts, all of Mumma's children will stand on their side of the court and watch the mah jong balls bounce in bounds, just slightly beyond them, and roll out of bounds. No ones tries to run after and return even one ball.

And Mumma's children will invent their own Home Rules combination of Hearts, Poker, and Go Fish, fish your wish, flowers (as Jane classifies them) are wild, round coinies count double. And, unless you go for Power and have all the red swords with the box in the middle, you will be up the creek, a thirteen-point penalty for each one.

"Dad, you've barely even got a hand. That just counts up to two, maybe four points," Tom will say.

"No. I won," Dad will reply, "This game you kids play makes no sense. Mah jong has been around for generations. The seasons are not flowers. I told you kids, you just have to pay attention."

"No, ours is better, Dad," Tom will say, "Ours is fun."

"Fun? It's not supposed to be fun, you're supposed to be learning something!" Dad will shake his head, and folding and pocketing the sheet of hand-drawn mah jong rules he made for the kids, he will walk away, leaving them to play with the tiles on the dining room table. The last thing Dad will hear is Jane saying, "Yay! I get to play! Flowers are wild. I'll play Dad's hand. How do you play again?"

"Mumma," he will say, joining Mumma in the kitchen, "when Janie is old enough, sign her up for community league tennis lessons, OK? I'm not going to teach her."

"Can do," Mumma replies, Wing calling his own wife, Mumma, for so many years, she doesn't even notice anymore.

Dad will never get the Home Rules right. And Mumma's kids will never play his rules of the game, God knows what those characters on the tiles actually mean.

And Jane will want to keep the tiles with the flowers for her own rituals.

And the bear will never come down. Over the years, the bear will get mangy-looking, covered with snow in winter, matted and grey during spring thaw. He will rock a bit in the wind, but other than that will not move.

And words are never spoken, never heard on those Sundays beneath the bear, out the non-basement, mah jong window.

And down from the pawn shop, around the corner from the bear, the new parking space for the taking it easy getaway onto Jasper Avenue is a great parking space where the Lees will become accustomed to parking.

"I guess this is not bad," Dad will say, making a smooth, slightly accelerating right turn onto Jasper Avenue.

"It's only a couple more blocks. Really," Mumma will reply, the windows of W.W. Arcade disappearing from sight in a fluid arc.

And on that car ride home, as they approach the flatiron building each Communion Sunday after crossing the path of the bear, twice, Mumma will pretend not to notice the empty handle of the Coffee Cup Inn, will pretend that she doesn't still see the man lying like an upside-down "V" in the handle.

And on Communion Sunday but only on Communion Sunday, the Lees will hear eight unseen hands perpetuate the ritual of the circle, and the bear will hold out its hands and transmit from its open mouth, wordless sounds from the room at the back.

Number 88. Spicy Beef in Lettuce Wraps

How can Auntie Moe stand living with a grave-in-waiting? How can she take it? That's what I want to know. I think about that every time we go to the Chinese cemetery. Auntie Moe is Mumma's baby sister and she doesn't drive, so Mumma and I drive her, once a month, on school days off, as long as there isn't fresh snow on the roads.

Auntie Moe is cool. She buys me "cutting edge" clothes for my birthday. Lately, she's started wearing miniskirts under her midi coat. And vinyl boots with square heels. Boots when it isn't snowing or even raining outside. Auntie Moe dresses so "with it," she wears cool bangs like Lulu, and frosty eye shadow. So what's she doing with a grave-in-waiting?

That's what's on our minds as we stand in front of Uncle Louie's gravestone. Gross. A big dark grey stone, bigger than most of the ones around it. The left side of the stone says *Chan Gee Gum Kwee*, underneath that *Born May 20, 1911* and underneath that *Died March 13, 1965*. All the lettering chiselled right out of the stone, and the insides of the letters and numbers painted white. So the stone doesn't just say things, it says them forever. Underneath the dates, a bunch of Chinese writing in four long columns, saying God knows what. But the right side of the stone says *Maureen Lily Chan*, and underneath that *Born July 23, 1938 —*. The rest of that side, shiny, polished, grey-grey blank. I ate a sandwich before we came, but seeing Auntie Moe's name and birthday, and all that blankness on her side of the gravestone makes me rub my hand across my tummy. Feels like thick, greasy noodles lumping up under my warm hand. Auntie Moe stands there, her mouth an upside-down sausage painted frosty pink. In her left hand, Mumma balances garden shears, a water jug's handle, and some yellow dahlias from home. Her right hand grips Auntie Moe's. But like always, Mumma lets go of Auntie Moe's hand, squeezes her around the shoulder, and says, "Well, the sooner we start."

Then, and this part always kills me, Mumma will walk straight up to the stone, right over that big rectangle of ground that any fool can see rests slightly lower than all the ground around it. The grass almost looks the same, but dips down in a rectangle. And even that grass rectangle leans a little bit more to the left than centre. Come to think of it, the firm ground to the right, the Auntie Moe side, where the grass grows on the same level as the rest of the world, makes it even more of a puzzle as to what Auntie Moe's doing with a grave-in-waiting. But how can Mumma do that, walk right over a rectangle of the dead? Me, I can't even put my toes near the edges. I get dizzy thinking about it. *That* dirt is softer, shifting. Restless. I know that dirt will move. Dirt isn't solid powder. Dirt is little round pebbles, marbles that will roll, give way to running shoes and eight-year-old legs. This is serious stuff, not just walking on sidewalk cracks. Even Auntie Moe, who married Uncle Louie, stands outside the foot of the rectangle and watches Mumma lower herself down, her hand holding the top of the tombstone for balance. Mumma plucks dry, straw-brown flowers from last time out of two green cone-shaped metal vases. The vases have big coat-hanger wire stems that push into the ground. Mumma pulls the vases right out of the ground, turns to me and Auntie Moe, smiling. "Well?"

Auntie Moe, who hasn't said one word, has her arms wrapped around her. She walks along the left edge and crouches down beside my mom, who squats dead centre at the top of the rectangle.

Mumma washes out the vases with a little water from her jug. She dampens a rag and starts to rub at the bird poop on the stone. Auntie Moe still has her arms wrapped around her as she rocks on her square heels. Auntie Moe has excellent balance.

"Well, run along," Mumma says to me.

Right. Like I'm going to run in the cemetery, let my feet step all over these grave tops. Sure. Maybe it's just her way of saying, "Get lost," but with Mumma, maybe the obvious just doesn't occur to her.

I don't mind. I heel toe heel toe heel toe along the higher ridges of grass. The ridges are continuous and they intersect, sideways with up and down. They make a grid pattern, like streets on a city map, each gravestone a sort-of house with a sunken front yard. Flowers nod in the breeze in front some of the gravestones, real flowers and fake ones too. A few grave-stones have oranges and incense and burnt papers with Chinese writing scattered in front. And almost empty Crown Royal whisky bottles that, Mumma says, are not left by drunks and are filled with coloured water. I picked one up once and it smelled like the real thing. All the stones have a flat polished front with those chiselled-in figures. Almost all have dates. Some with Chinese writing only, some with English writing only, and some with both.

I read as I walk along. If there are dates, sometimes I do the math. *Jonathan Wong Gee, Born December 22, 1949, Died December 29, 1959.* Oh. Ten years old. That's so sad. There's a bunch of little oranges set out in front of the stone. Sad oranges. And babies too, six months, or eighteen months. When I come across the skinny little baby gravestones, I don't do math, or even read them anymore. I count clouds, keep an ear out for bees. Or, I pull at my hangnails and keep walking. Here's one of my favourites, *Wee Lee, Born October 21, 1901, Died April 10, 1959.* Fifty-seven. And the last little piggy went Wee Lee all the way home. I laugh, but quickly stop. I look down and just watch my feet walking. Right left right left. Right beside Wee Lee, there's one of those gravestones with a photograph, like a cameo locket, embedded in the centre. Once I know where those photo ID gravestones are, I just keep moving. I get prickly ears looking at the little photos. Because now I've got a face for who's underneath that rectangle of grass.

Looking up the hill, I can see Mumma and Auntie Moe talk-ing. Auntie Moe hasn't moved, still crouching, hugging herself. She talks when Mumma's hands stop moving. The flowers lie beside Mumma's feet. So do the green metal vases.

Uncle Louie was way older than Auntie Moe, even older than my Dad. Really tall, and skinny — Uncle Louie's skin looked like yellowed wax paper. He kind of looked like what Herman Munster would look like if Herman Munster was Chinese. Yeah. Chinese Herman Munster. He wore a man's felt hat, even in the house, and always had bruise-coloured rings around his eyes. I can picture him, hitting the top of their old console television, then backing up slowly, eyes glued to the screen, until the back of his legs reached that flesh-tone La-Z-Boy and his knees would bend to sitting. Wearing that hat. Looking at the wide white television tower, just outside the cemetery, I have the idea that Uncle Louie must be doing OK.

On that TV tower side of the graveyard, someone built a shrine, this garden shed with a hexagon-shaped Chinese-y looking roof and, instead of walls, four support beams and a wide wooden ledge running all the way around it at my eye level. Every single time we pass the shrine, leaving the cemetery, I say to Mumma, "Slow down. Slow. Down." From the car, I can see burnt paper banners with Chinese writing hanging down from the ledge. And sitting on top of the ledge, I love seeing the little glass cups filled with amber liquid, oranges, incense sticks, and red paper envelopes for lucky money. I'd like to check out this great stuff, but right beside the shrine is where they bury the recently dead. No grass on the rectangles, no gravestones. Just lots of flowers, or paper banners laying over soft, rounded piles of dirt. Fresh graves.

I keep walking. The farther along I go, the longer the tombstones have been here. Here's a double. On the Uncle Louie side, probably the man, *Wah Keen Sang, 1953 minus 1890*. Sixty-three. And, *Wah Ng Lee, 1963 minus 1891*. Seventy-two. Good on her. Old Wah waited, let's see, ten years, which is nothing when you compare that to poor old Ng Lee having a grave-in-waiting for the same period of time.

Bits have cracked off some of these gravestones. Lots have rusty cauliflower-looking crud stuck on them, where the paint on the letters has chipped away. Some just have one date on them, like 1924, and a bunch of Chinese writing. Or no dates at all. Out here, No Vacancy, all the double graves are full up. Words and numbers chiselled on both sides. No more waiting. Hardly any flowers or oranges or little red envelopes by the gravestones, even the sad ones.

We don't put oranges, or incense sticks, booze, or Chinese fake Monopoly money out for Uncle Louie. On account of God. We don't do ancestor worship, Mumma says, because we believe in God. I'm not going to ask Mumma, but what about the graves where there's oranges and incense *and* flowers and chiselled-in words about God? Mumma would say that's called dealing from both ends of the deck.

I think about God near the end or I guess the beginning, the boundary, of the Chinese graveyard. I don't think about Him much at church. We go to the Chinese United Church and the whole service is in Chinese. I don't understand word one. It's mostly old Chinese people. Hymn singing sounds like everyone got their hair caught in a revolving door. Lizzie says the reason's because something-something Chinese music has a five-note scale and Western music has an eight-note scale, but that's not true. What an excuse. People just don't know how to sing in tune. After and before, the old ladies pinch your cheeks and ask you things in Chinese. Then they repeat the question. You stress smile, which hurts your cheeks all the way up to your eyeballs, until Mumma says something in Chinese. Then everyone laughs, including Mumma. I can't stand it, the worst sixty-minute hour in the world. But my point is, out here, alone, surrounded by these sunken rectangles of the dead and chiselled words like *The Lord Is My Shepherd* and *He Is Risen*, well, He occupies my mind.

Across the cemetery road at the Ukrainian cemetery, their stones are massive, six feet tall. They have graves-in-waiting too. Some of the gravestones have just one word, a name, as far as I can see. *Kureluk, Holubitsky*. And sometimes that word isn't spelled in the English alphabet, but the alphabet with the little curlicues and backwards image letters. The Ukrainians are buried in one cemetery, and on the other side of the street, here's all the Chinese.

And it comes to me all at once, I work out how God and religion and the afterlife fit together. When you die, you go to heaven, sure. But, you live in heaven with the people you're buried with. That's why the graves-in-waiting. Like putting a sweater on the seat beside you at the movie theatre while your mumma is out buying the popcorn. It's just saving a space no one else can push their bum, well, their whole bod into.

The traffic whizzes by on the other side of the cement barrier. The sunlight shines on the bare branches of the trees, the leaves long gone, and I have that warm feeling from figuring something out, like learning how to add fractions. But suddenly, the rows and rows of tombstones in the Chinese cemetery help me figure something else out. One day, I'm going to spend the rest of eternity with a bunch of old Chinese people who don't speak English. It will be like going to church every day for the rest, no, beyond the rest of my life. I mean, this is where they bury the Chinese-Canadians. Everyone in my heaven will be Chinese, and hardly anyone will speak English. They won't have had to speak English for years, so they'll have lost it. We Lee kids are, as Grandpa holds over our heads, the only Chinese kids in the entire city who don't really know word one of Chinese. My stomach twinges. My armpits feel warm and greasy. What if I get there before Mumma or Dad, who will interpret?

What kind of heaven is this anyway?

"Shake a leg, Janie! We're going."

My feet come off the ground. Mumma waves her garden shears at me. Auntie Moe brushes dust off her coat sleeves. "Janie. C'mon."

I sit in the backseat beside Mumma's garden tools. The inside of the car smells like mud and peat moss.

"Mumma, just for instance," I throw out, casual as can be, "If I happened to die, I guess this is where you'd bury me, right?"

Mumma turns around and gives me her you-gotta-be-kidding-me look. "You worry too much," she says, turning back to pay attention to her driving, "You're as healthy as a horse, Janie. You're going to outlive and outrun us all. No one's planning a funeral any time soon."

Ha. So I am right. My eyes burn holes in the back of the driver's seat. What kind of people would bury a non-Chinese-speaking Canadian child in the Chinese graveyard?

Auntie Moe sits as far away from Mumma as she can in the front seat. We're driving her home to Grandpa's. Auntie Moe works at Village Books on Thursday and Friday nights and all day Saturday. She takes the bus there and back. Whenever I'm out with Mumma and Dad at night and see those buses riding around, all lit up inside with one or two passengers sitting by themselves, I think of Auntie Moe.

I have no idea why she moved to Grandpa's when Uncle Louie died. Well, he's her father and everything, but he's such a grump. He looks exactly like the porcelain Buddha doll Dad's cousins in Saskatoon prop in front of their fireplace. He's got the round, round bald head, little square white teeth with brown edges, and the jiggly fat of an enormous gut and floppy breasts. In the summer, when Grandpa wears just undershirts, you can even see those little dots around his nipples, just like the Buddha doll's. But that Buddha doll sits there with these children climbing all over him, and I don't know any kid who'd come near Grandpa. And not just because his breath would knock a cow over. You don't have to spend much time with him to realize he is just plain mean. He doesn't know much English, but what he knows is pick-pick-pick. You'll be over visiting, having a chat with Auntie Moe, and he'll be talking with your Dad, and all of a sudden, he'll interrupt you to say, "Aiya. Childen. Be Seeing. Not Hearing." If he were that Buddha doll, he'd be swatting those kids away like flies. But one thing about Grandpa. At least his daughters can speak Chinese. They're all set. It feels like someone is dragging a teabag soaked in vinegar across the bottom of my stomach.

"You're quiet today, Little One." Auntie Moe turns and smiles at me from the front seat of the car. If a storybook mother who likes kids came to live in your life, she would be my Auntie Moe. "What are you thinking?"

"Mmmm. Nothing."

I wish I said, something. Auntie Moe shrugs her shoulders and turns around again.

"Well, what are you thinking about?" I ask.

"Nothing too."

"Next month, maybe Auntie Moe will have time to go out for tea," I hear from the back of Mumma's head.

"I don't think we need to do this any more," Auntie Moe says, looking straight ahead.

"Well, we'll keep an eye on the weather," Mumma says.

"No." I lean forward, I can hardly hear Auntie Moe. "I mean any more."

"Oh?" Mumma has that bug-eyed tone that means she's not really asking.

"Brian says this just prolongs the mourning period —"

"Who's Brian?" I ask, perching my chin over the seat edge.

"— I told him, three years, mourning isn't what it's about. But he has a point."

"Maybe," Mumma says, "maybe Brian doesn't understand Duty. Or loyalties."

"Who's Brian?"

"I explained all that to him, but Brian says it sounds like I'm doing this more for Dad," Auntie Moe turns her face toward Mumma, "and you, Mary."

"Oh. Well. You tell Brian, you don't owe me anything. All this time, I thought hey, just helping you. But if you don't want to do this anymore, you tell Brian I'm not going to drag you to the cemetery each month, kicking and screaming. I don't need to help you and then have you tell me you're the one doing me a favour."

"Who is Brian?"

(one-two-three-) The front seat goes Chinese. Like the film at school on the UN Assembly, your translation headset cuts out. And then all you hear is Chinese.

This happens all the time at the juicy bits. I watch, like a tennis match, with my eyes following the ball of words being slugged back and forth between Auntie Moe and Mumma. I think Chinese people sometimes sound like they're arguing, but I don't need a translator to know this is the real thing.

I listen in case one word, one syllable will turn sideways for a second, reveal its insides, and meaning to me. But they talk so fast, the words pour out like jelly beans from a jar. "Brian" peppered through the Chinese. I listen harder. Wait.

My head hurts. They could be talking about space travel, Astronaut Brian, and freeze-dried food in foil packets. And, if I don't learn Chinese, my heaven will become this — watching tennis matches of people talking back and forth to each other, endless buckets of balls made of words I don't understand. That'll be me, Janie Lee, heaven's permanent spectator who has Nothing to Say and No One Talking to Her. Worse. I'll starve. I don't even know how to ask how to find the bathroom. I wonder if I'll have to go in heaven.

Already in front of Grandpa's house. We usually stop and visit, but Mumma squeezes the life out of what Dad calls the 10 and 2 of the steering wheel, and the car engine rumbles.

"I'll call you," Auntie Moe says, "See ya."

"Mmm."

"See ya, Auntie Moe."

Mumma takes off without letting me come up to the front. The whole ride home she doesn't speak Chinese or English. I pretend to point and say, "I don't care for that, and I don't care for that, nor that either. None of it," I silently conclude, my hand pretending to sweep the air clear, "Please take it all away." I am a lady of leisure being driven home by her cranky chauffeur.

....

"How was school today?"

"There wasn't any school. We went to the cemetery."

At dinner tonight, you can hear the knives and forks click clack against the plates. Three of us sit in the kitchen. Everyone else is at Boy Scouts, or drama club, or a late class. While Mumma made supper, I went downstairs to the den and took down these old paperbacks of Dad's with all Chinese writing. They sat in the den in the little gold metal bookcase. I tried to figure out the squiggly characters, looking for patterns, repeated figures. Maybe if I broke the code, those squiggles and lines could move on the page, form letters spelling words with the English alphabet.

"What have you got there?"

I didn't know Dad had already come home. When I looked up, end-of-the-day light shone through the basement windows. And my legs felt cold on the floor where I sat, my fingers running lines over the writing.

"Just some old books."

"Anything interesting?" He put his chin over my shoulder.

"Not really."

"Might be more interesting if you start at the beginning of the book, not the end." He moved the pages from under my fingers.

"Oh?"

"And each page," he said, running his fingers to the bottom of the page, "you read the rows top to bottom, right to left."

"Oh."

....

Mumma dabs the napkin at the corners of her mouth, signalling me to clear the table.

"Yes," she says, "we went to the cemetery today." The Chinese starts again. Even sounds like the same conversation, like a needle on a sewing machine madly piercing the fabric, "de-de-de-de-de-de-de-Brian-de-de-de-de-de-de-Brian-de-de-de."

Dad massages his jaw with his left hand. He talks. A question? I stand between them, my hands curved around the plates stacked at the table. The tennis ball of words flips back and forth, over me, I first think, like a net. Then, through me. I frown at this sample of bad heaven.

"de-de-de-de."

"What are you talking about?"

"de-de-de-de-de-de-de-de-de-de."

"Who's Brian?"

"de-de-de-de-de-de-de-de-de-de —"

"What are you talking about?"

"de-de-de-de-de-de —"

"I said. What are you talking about?"

"Clear the dishes."

"You heard Mumma. Clear the dishes."

"Will you at least answer my question? Who is Brian?"

"Young lady!"

"You always talk Chinese. You know I don't understand —"

"Hold your horses, Janie —"

"You talk right in front of me. That's rude."

"Go to your room." Mumma points down the hall.

....

I had this terrible dream last night. Four old Chinese men I never met, playing mah jong in a kitchen I never saw before. The one facing me didn't say a word, but I knew it was Wee Lee, bugging his eyes at me. They sat around a card table, shirt sleeves rolled up, mah jong tiles arranged in long rows piled two high in front of each person. The right-hand end of each row of mah jong tiles butted up against the mid-point of the row of tiles to each player's right, the four rows forming a smaller square of mah jong tiles with pinwheel ends. The men smoked cigarettes, but I only smelled incense burning. Each man had a small glass of whisky set on the table in front of him, and when Wee Lee pointed at me with his chin, the other three all turned. Speaking in Chinese (the good part of the dream was that I could understand Chinese), Wee Lee pointed his finger at my face, and whined loudly, "She doesn't know any Chinese." The other three gave me the hairy eyeball. One of the men closest to me pushed his chair back from the table, stood up. "Shame!" he cried, shaking a handful of thin white papers at me. Then the rest stood up and joined him, yelling in Chinese, "You don't belong here! Shame, shame! Get out!" I started to run, and they jumped up, scattering their chairs. They began to chase me, throwing little oranges at my head. An orange hit me in the head, I tripped, and kept falling. I screamed. Out loud, I think. My eyes opened. My hair felt hot and stuck on, like a rubber bathing cap. I had a droolly pillow and crusts in my eyes. Sweaty under my jeans and long-sleeved tee shirt. The whole house had gone to bed. Quiet. And dark. No one came to check on me, for a pulse, or anything. I got up and changed in the dark.

....

All day long, I have ridden in the back seat, not saying a word. Everyone else has swimming, piano lessons, homework. The people in the front seat have finished all their Saturday driving errands. What I don't get is when you are a grown-up and can finally do whatever you want, how do you end up doing so much boring stuff all day long? That won't be me, ever. They make a point of speaking English all day, turning their heads toward the back seat as if to include me. I'm no fool. What they're talking about isn't important. And I haven't been listening. The car stops at Pinder's house. Mumma went to school with Barbara Pinder, who still lives at home, taking care of her mother. Just the two of them, mother and daughter. My shoulders quiver and the shaking travels right down my back. The Pinders live about three blocks from Village Books, where Auntie Moe works today.

I slam the car door shut. "I'm going to the bookstore," I say.

"Janie, where are you going?" Mumma asks. She doesn't even listen.

"Let her go," Dad says. "Call us at the Pinder's and we'll come get you. Jane?"

"Mmm."

....

Auntie Moe works at the counter, helping a customer. He has his back to me, and he leans over so she doesn't see me come in. There's no one else in the store. I'm not to bother her while she's working, so I browse a shelf of books off to one side. She still doesn't see me.

Is she arm wrestling? They both have their elbows on the counter and their fingers make a big ball fist. But, Auntie Moe makes a pretty puny arm wrestler. He could easily win, and yet they're just, I don't know, checking out each other's nostrils or something. Wait. He wraps his other hand around and lifts their ball fist to his face. Don't tell me they're making goo-goo eyes. Hey. He kisses her knuckles. Each one separately. Gross. And better than television. She smiles and turns her head toward me.

The way Auntie Moe's head and my head both move back, you can tell we're related. She undoes her hand from the ball. I don't know what to do. Or say. She waves me over. He turns to face me. He's very tall.

"Jane, this is my friend, Brian. Brian, this is my favourite eight-year-old niece, Jane."

"Your only eight-year-old niece," I correct.

"But, still my favourite." Our routine.

His camel's hair coat goes on forever. But he has soft grey-brown eyebrows and long eyelashes like a pony. His smile crinkles his eyes. The point of his nose matches the points of his shoes matches the blunt tips of his outstretched fingers. The ones that were so close to his lips.

He has warm hands.

"What's up, Little One?" Auntie Moe asks. She looks so pinky clear.

"I need to talk to you," I whisper.

I like Brian. Without asking, he wanders off to the shelves.

"Why so glum, chum?"

Auntie Moe crosses her arms on the counter and her head tilts in a paying attention way. She should be a mother.

"Auntie Moe, I need to learn Chinese."

"Oh. Right away?"

"Well, I think that would be best. You never know when you'll need it."

"It's not so easy, you know. What do you need to learn first?"

"Well, like, 'Where is the bathroom?' and 'Do you have chicken sandwiches?' and 'Go away. I don't know.' Like that."

"Come with me," she says. We walk by Brian to a bookcase with a sign that says Travel. Auntie Moe picks a book off the lowest shelf, and hands it to me, *Berlitz Chinese for Travellers: A 40-Page Guide.*

"You're lucky," she says, "Not many of these around."

The book cover shines in my hands. The cream-coloured pages feel thick between my fingers. There's a column of phrases in English, and then another column, English letters spelling Chinese words. I try one out as we walk slowly back to the counter.

"Joh Sun."

"Good morning to you too," Auntie Moe gently tugs a piece of hair by my bangs, "but you're about eight hours late —"

"I knew that," I shout, "Yes, good morning. I knew that."

Then Auntie Moe reaches under the counter and takes her wallet out. "Don't worry," she says, punching the till buttons, "your early Christmas present." She flips the clip down on the dollar bills and fishes some coins out of the little compartments.

....

The three of us ride in Brian's car. Dad said OK. First, we'll go out for spaghetti and then play it by ear, Auntie Moe says. I sit in the back seat. The car has leather upholstery that smells like forever. They reach across the front seat and hold hands.

"Or, we could go get doughnuts," Auntie Moe says.

"Or, we could go bowling," Brian says.

"Or, we could drive out to the Stardust Drive-in, park off the road, and make up the dialogue for the actors on the screen."

Every idea sounds better than the last one. I fold the paper bag carefully around my book, and hold on with both hands. As Auntie Moe and Brian make plans, all of a sudden I start thinking about Uncle Louie. What would it be like, you tell everyone in heaven that you're waiting for someone, "Yup, she's coming," you say, but no one ever shows up. I mean, you're there for eternity, and all your heaven friends know you're waiting, and you know everyone knows you're waiting, duh, because you were the one who told them. But no one ever comes. How can Uncle Louie stand waiting for eternity like that? That's what I want to know.

Number 183. Seafood-Steam Whitefish with Scallion Chop

Vee's eyes revel in the silver of the mirror, awe-struck by Vee's reflection. The world could be mapped from the precision of her lips, the true north of the identical twin peaks drawn at the centre of her Pink Frost lips. Round light bulbs necklace the oval mirror on the new, white vanity. Pink light catches flecks of airborne sparkle from Vee herself. You could argue (but not with Vee) that the true source of this dust may be Vee's powder puff and engraved sterling compact.

Kohl eyeliner traces her almond-shaped eyes, the nut-shaped stencil borrowed from Vee by Elizabeth Taylor in the movie, *Cleopatra*. Vee gloriaswansons her eyes, combs her right, then left Kissmequick eyelashes, a doll-sized toothbrush held between the tips of her thumb and forefinger. Two rows of lashes stand at attention. On the mark. Blink. Hello, Chatelaine of Contemporary Style.

Vee grinds her slipper heels against the hardwood and pushes back, the wheels on her round tufted stool rolling hard against the veneer of the floor. Delighted to see more of her body materializing in the mirror, Vee concentrates on her mirror image as she crosses her legs, right over left, and wrists, left over right, manicured fingertips resting tentatively on top of her right thigh. She gently pats her hairline around her forehead, before re-posing her hands on her thigh. Orange sherbet pedal pushers cut just below her calves, matching her sleeveless pop top. Invisible zippers in the side seams of both garments flatter her you-can-crack-an-egg-on-my-ass figure. A gold slipper with a courtier heel swings from the ball of her foot, pivoting a slender ankle. A band of gold and white holds a long, thick ponytail in place at the top of her head. Vee twirls her head in the style of Nancy Kwan, her neck snapping smartly just behind her right ear, the ponytail a black lasso circling her shoulders.

Nancy Kwan, singer, dancer, actress. All-American. Movie star. Nancy Kwan, in the movie *Flower Drum Song*, telling the world, singing, that "She Flips when a fella brings her flowers." That "She is strictly a female female." That "She Enjoys being a Girl." *Flower Drum Song*, those real life alluring characters, speaking directly to glamourous Vee. Oriental men wearing fedoras and talking fast, regular so-handsome-they-make-your-bits-quiver guys. Snapping their fingers. Cool movie star Chinese guys. And not just one or two guys. OhNo. Chorus lines of adagio dancing, singing, strutting, HelloGorgeous, guys. Living every day life in real time. Today. Wearing their handsome hearts on the sleeves of really well-cut suits. The leading men? Bedroom Eyes? Please. Just Like Michael Caine. Almond-shaped Michael Caine Bedroom Eyes. Regular matinee idols. No fat thugs. No skinny-rat-greaseball gangsters. None of that Charlie Chan narrow-eyed ohhh velly interesting ah so — asshole Oriental stuff. Nope. None of that, thank you. Just your run of the mill good-looking Oriental men. Oh, yes please. Real guys you can actually picture between you and the ceiling. Vee crosses her arms, her shoulders shrug, finger tips stroke the sides of her breasts.

Vee frowns. Fantasy always poses a challenge. Has to start with a wedding, Vee's no floozie-tart. Guy's got to smell good, like cinnamon bark, fresh coconut, or lime leaves. He has to have nice teeth, lots of money, and be Chinese. At least Oriental. With the good eyes. [Note: God knows how the epicanthal fold can put a hitch in some people's giddy-up.] Vee hates how she bourgeoisifies her fantasy life, but she can't help it. There's the list, and all the ingredients need to be added. She's tried to negotiate some of the variables, find an express lane, a round the back shortcut, a quick beginning with the end in mind. But the fantasy just does not go anywhere, even in her head, let alone lower. Since marrying Malmo four years ago, well, the rules absolutely had to change — fantasy now has to start with Vee as a widow, wild with grief and not responsible for her behaviour.

It's not a betrayal, just fantasy. To be pragmatic and, well, in a way loving, Vee has come upon a shorthand preamble that sees Malmo disappearing on a business trip to San Francisco, something about costing out contingencies. Vee obtains an official declaration of her presumed widowhood, expedited by a very compassionate Korean man at the Canadian Consulate in S.F. His teeth line up like tight Chiclets, the brown-eyed man in a well-cut suit who embosses Vee's declaration. Vee's permit, a presumption of widowhood that gets tossed over her mental shoulder when Vee hears the motor on the garage door at the end of Malmo's work day.

In the oval-shaped vanity mirror at the edge of Vee's reflection, you can see a wall painted and textured Alabaster Frost. Shimmery white with an undertone of candy pink. You can also see part of the back of a gilt-edged chaise longue, upholstered in white silk damask, a subtle pattern of gardenia buds and ivy leaves. On the other side of the mirror, a spindle bedpost at the foot of the bed pins a coordinating white damask bedspread. Vee saw *Flower Drum Song* seventeen times including matinees at Edmonton's Paramount Theatre on Jasper Avenue. Taking notes the last five times. Taking Malmo the last two times. Vee rotates slowly on her stool, surveying in a fan-shaped line, the rest of her newly renovated bedroom from the raised, circular platform where her vanity sits. In the *Flower Drum Song* movie dream sequence, Nancy Kwan's Strictly-A-Female-Female bridal salon-white bedroom transforms into her fantasy married life bedroom, decorated with sheer white curtains suspended from the ceiling and covering nothing in particular, Greek columns, and a white bedroom suite. Malmo agreed that Vee could have everything the same in their own bedroom but not the columns. And he wouldn't buy a new mattress for the bed — Vee finds Malmo cheap about kooky things. From her brand new circular platform, Vee recalls how she went back and forth on the white leather Wassily chairs, loved them, then concluded that the tubular chrome chairs with white walls breathing a pink undertone into the space would make the bedroom lean more o.b./gynie than tony/upscale. No Wassily, what a great decision Vee thinks, confident that she stopped just short of ostentatious.

Vee's homage to Nancy. Nancy Kwan. Vee swivels to face the mirror, her reflection smiles back. A woman. Pink, and Rich. Sassy. Marabou-feathered. Chinese. And No Accent. No Rs for Ls, No "No Speakee Engarish." None of that. Until Nancy Kwan, Vee felt a bit betrayed by her relationship with Hollywood. Stoic peasant women in coolie hats, attempting to pass themselves off as The Chinese Women, what the hell does Pearl S. Buck know about being Chinese. Academy Award-winning *The Good Earth*, my ass — like everyone was born in a rice paddy, for God's sake.

....

Malmo lies awake in the middle of the night, wondering how he came to be sleeping in, yah, and paying big bucks, to be sleeping in a giant God damned toilet bowl. Clean, yes. Plenty of Sparkle. Still, a God damned giant white toilet bowl. The oval mirror on Vee's vanity brings to mind shake-tuck-zip-flush-put-the-seat-down. The five-hundred-dollar-apiece gauzy white curtains pooling on the floor say giant reams of t.p.

He saw the movie. Cringed in his seat as Vee kept hitting his arm with the back of her hand, whispering, "See this. Oh, yeah, *this* is thepart, this is thepart. Ohhh. That. *That* too. See *this*? Thispart. Yeah. Yeah. That's what I want." This went on through the whole movie — twice — but it's still not clear to Malmo what exactly Vee wanted to show him. Except the bedroom. That was clear. Small mercy, the rest of Nancy Kwan's dream sequence apartment was nondescript, a hallway with lots of doors and a kitchen with a round tan leather banquette.

Malmo turns on his right side, Vee's hair loose waves on the pillow beside his. He strokes the ends of her long black hair. Did she see the kids in the dream sequence, having seen the film, what, nine times? She must have seen the kids. Malmo smiles. He remembers the kids as the absolute highlight of the movie for him, the movie verifying Malmo's concept drawings of fatherhood: two kids, an older boy and a little girl burst through a hallway door; those mischievous but good scamps run down the hall and out a different hallway door, their great-looking mother following; the two kids grow up, do well in school, come through the hallway door again as bopping teenagers and disappear out another door. They listen to their father. Respect him. The kids become a credit to him, bring honour to the family. Check, check, double check.

Like Uncle Wing's kids. "I want to be a marine biologist," six-year-old Tom says, taking Malmo by the hand to the back of the store. There are no windows in the back, but a wooden wedge props the door to the lane open. A pool of soft light warms the back of the store, but near the door, the dark of the lane absorbs the light. [Note: A solitary bulb suspended from the ceiling with a piece of butcher string dangling as a pull cord might inspire an inventor six years from now to market the home dimmer switch.]

At the back of Wing's store, it smells like damp wood, sweet with soda pop, rows of pop bottles stacked in cardboard crates. On top of a wooden table, a battleship linoleum tile with gold flecks trivets a bowl aquarium full of activity. An inch of black-and-white aquarium gravel makes a foundation for the home of two orange swordtail fish.

"They breathe from this," Tom says, pointing to the bubbling blue plastic sea diver taking up most of the space in the bowl, "and Dad says if these guys live, like, make it through the whole week, I might get more on the weekend. Maybe a neon tetra." Tom floats a fourth pinch of tiny brown and copper coloured flakes on the lens of the water. The fish shimmy to the top of the bowl, mouths breaking the surface.

"Dad says don't squeeze them when they're pooping. That'll kill them."

Tom puts his hand on top of Malmo's. "Uncle Malmo. You can't even hold them. Or pet them. Because they'll lose their scales. Dad says that'll kill them too."

Dad says. Wing is at least twenty years older than Malmo, from the same village. Wing left as a child, alone, and Malmo, escaping the Japanese invasion, decades later. Wing treats Malmo like a kid brother, and Malmo's always hanging around the store, showing Wing his new stuff, taking Wing under the hood of his new car, showing Wing the cuffs and deep pleats of Malmo's custom-made suits.

"'You Call Everybody Darling', you know that song?" Vee says one night at dinner. "'You call everybody Uncle,'" Vee sings, "'Everybody calls you Uncle too.'"

Malmo can't figure out how Wing manages. Well, there's his wife. But he's old and he's got all those young kids, and that little go-nowhere store downtown on Rice Street. And no education. But he makes it. Malmo's a university graduate, a Civil Engineer. But Malmo's the little brother around Wing, always one step behind. How does a six-year-old know what a marine biologist is?

Those kids in the movie were fantastic, Malmo thinks. Great kids.

Malmo moves closer to Vee, his hand cups her bony hip as his striped pyjama pants spoon her bare legs. Their combined lower body weight on the mattress makes Malmo feel as if his feet have passed the lip and are sliding downward towards the small end of a funnel. The urgency compels Malmo to move closer, his pyjama pants drawing tighter, until the lawnmowers in Vee's sinuses rev to starting.

She's out. The telephone beside the bed, the white phone that lights up when it rings, wouldn't even wake her now. Malmo flips over to his left side, curls his right arm against the cold lip of the funnel.

"No new mattress," he said to Vee. One of those details he had meant to take care of, should have taken care of, before they married, the mattress one he had had all through university and those early years as a Civil Engineer. They really should have had a new mattress when they got married. But they didn't. And now, No new mattress until Vee finished weaning the first baby boy, a village custom. He didn't tell Vee that.

....

The *Edmonton Journal* came to photograph Vee and Malmo in their newly designed bedroom for the Homes Section a couple of weeks ago. The *Journal* graciously provided Vee and Malmo with a framed print of the photo that would run with the article. The photographer loved "the draping, all the draping," "the light, the interplay of light and shadow," "the subtlety of the contrast white with white."

The Saturday next, those are the words The *Journal* will use liberally in the article, which will also describe Vee and Malmo as a "professional couple about town." Vee will buy twenty-seven copies of that Saturday's paper, then crack open a bottle of champagne Saturday night, which neither of them will drink, Vee hating the bubbles in her nose. Malmo likes bubbles, but just in pilsner.

The following Monday, Mr. Cheney, owner of the engineering firm where Malmo works, Mr. Cheney's large, cupped hand will clap Malmo on the shoulder and assert a firm grip of congratulations into his warm palm. Throughout the day, Malmo's colleagues will say, "Hey, I saw the article in the paper," and, "You guys don't have kids, do you, all that white," or, "Thanks a lot, now my wife has got it in her head to renovate, says if you guys can do it, so can we. Kidding aside, it looks like a great job." None of the women in the secretarial pool say anything, but they will sparkly eye and both-rows-of-teeth-bigsmile Malmo all day long. Florence Kay, at reception, will tell him that her mother thinks Vee and her good taste are lucky to be married to such a modern man. For Malmo, the encounters over the day will feel awkward, like getting credit for something he didn't do. Nevertheless, Malmo will lay the pelts of these stories at Vee's feet when he returns home that night.

....

Malmo has not adapted to falling asleep in a noisy room. He shakes Vee's shoulder. Her snoring idles, sputters for a few seconds, then the mowers turn decisively to the back lawn.

Malmo focuses on the giant white curtain hanging at an angle off the foot of the bed. A few days before the photographer's shoot, Malmo had picked up Uncle Wing, driven him to the house when Vee was out, to see the bedroom renovation and all the redecorating.

"Wow," Wing said, "Malmo, this is so modern. Current, and fancy like a movie set. And — this is so much, so much — work."

Wing moved his hand behind, but not touching one of the curtains, the shadow of his palm slowly descending.

"Expensive, huh. Geez, what the kids'd do to this," Wing exhales through the small fish-kiss of his mouth, a soundless whistle. His cupped palm squeezes Malmo's shoulder gently. "No one else has this!"

Back at the store, as he closed the passenger door on Malmo's navy blue Meteor, Wing, polishing a small spot of chrome by the open window with his thumb, said, "That's just great, Malmo. When they come to film you, don't look at that camera. And wear a dark suit, eh?"

Malmo sits upright in bed. He hadn't remembered that until now.

Malmo's memory scans his copy of the photographer's print that will appear in this Saturday's Homes section, front page. The image is all there in black and white. In the foreground of the picture, Vee sitting on her vanity stool, looking away from the camera, canary-fed contentment in white lounging pyjamas, the wrists and shawl collar soft with marabou feathers. The oval vanity mirror to her right, Malmo slightly to her left, behind her, in a white turtleneck, slacks, and white bucks, one hand on Vee's shoulder, the other holding his white belt — Malmo looking directly at the camera lens. In the background, the white chaise longue, the coved ceiling and curved walls, the bedspread, the whiteness of the many layers of draping.

Malmo fades behind himself, imagines himself and Wing looking at a picture of the world's largest God Damn giant white toilet bowl and the idiot, dead centre, who OK'd it. Lives in the bowl, becomes the bowl. Too stupid to know any better.

....

A month later, Malmo comes in from the alley to the back of the store, his legs erratic scissors. The first Wednesday afternoon of the month, Wing checks the wholesale invoices by supplier against his ledger and files the invoices. "Uncle Wing, I've got something to show you."

Wing looks up from his ledger, turns down the volume on his Bakelite radio. "Malmo, what's a good-looking guy like you doing in a place like this? Hey, what d'ya got there?"

They never do speak about the picture in the newspaper, Wing always having said, "I get sixty copies of the newspaper delivered every day. Do I ever have time to look at any of them?" The subject never comes up. Malmo finds excuses to come to the store, has done so for years. He needs a packet of Sen-Sen before a big meeting, or some lemons to help a scratchy throat. Every week or so, a paper bag of dried-up oranges, a half roll of mints, an unopened potato chip bag will get thrown into Malmo's garbage can from the trunk of his car. He brings his empties to the back of the store. After school, Tom pops empty soda bottles into the cardboard crates, stacks the crates three high and two deep, and then counts the crates. Malmo moves out of his way, stands beside the two orange swordtails and two, no three, neon tetras swimming, an inch of rainbow-coloured aquarium gravel at the bottom. The fish live in a rectangular aquarium now that covers all but the edges of the linoleum tile.

Malmo takes the scroll of papers from the crook of his elbow and unrolls them on top of the crated empties. Wing pins the papers with a metal two-hole punch and a large stapler laid on its side. Wing cups his chin with the palm of his hand as he leans across the papers.

The concept drawings are as dramatic as the sequential blue prints are detailed. "Wing, the floor's made of high quality, transparent Lucite, cantilevered by a modified radial matrix of steel joists," Malmo's pencil-leaded fingertips glide over the top drawing. "Through to the subfloor, we'll seal the joists with a white polymer resin so they're virtually invisible looking down at them — most will come up under the banquette. On the joists, I'll float a sprayed and galvanized fibreglass basin, custom poured, right to the walls, to fit under the floor." Malmo lifts the hole punch, and three pages roll, echo-curl to the stapler.

"Here. I've done the structural analysis and preliminary stress bearing weight calculations, for water volume, fill weight, pumps, metal contraction and expansion. I've contacted a filtration pump manufacturer in L.A. and they're sending a draft spec proposal; the trick is the volume to depth ratio." He pulls on the corner of the page, and it peels against the stapler.

"I thought about electric heating rods through the subfloor, which would also work to help warm the basement. But I wanted to use my education, on this one," Malmo says, index finger lightly tapping his left temple. "So, I've devised a heat exchange system. It uses the waste heat from the kitchen —

you know, fridge, stove, dishwasher, to keep the water in the basin heated. This will cost me nothing to run. Will actually save money on the heating bill." Malmo licks his three middle fingers, and unleashes another page to the stapler.

"Here. Where the thermocouple will sit, completely safe, with two emergency generators, here and here."

Wing smooths the rolled papers away from the stapler, pins the top drawing under the two-hole punch. He points at small ellipses drawn on top of what he thinks Malmo called the sub-floor. "These are fish?"

Malmo shakes his head at Wing. He spreads his hands over the drawings as if he were blessing them. "Well yeah, that's what I've been talking about. Not just fish, Uncle Wing. Koi."

Wing's lips disappear into his mouth, "Koi. Fancy carp. Why don't you just buy a big aquarium for your kitchen?"

"Because," Malmo says immediately, "I want a koi pond. I live in Canada, the West, I...I want a koi pond. A pond with koi because they're... koi. You remember them," Malmo says.

"No, not really. But I know what koi are."

"They're the best. And I want them."

The two men stare at each other, irises widening, cones and rods skimming the index file, needle scratching, skipping, wildly searching for the groove, any groove on the record.

Wing turns off the Bakelite radio. "If you want this, I want this for you."

"Tom could help," Malmo says, excitedly, "I'm going to need a marine biologist to help me chose the fish, Uncle."

"He'd like that, but you know, now he wants to be a magician."

....

[Notes:

1.   Anyone who knows about retrofit water-bearing structural designs and specifications will know that Malmo's design can create a technically perfect pool of water — water-tight, durable, filtered, aerated, competently supported.

2.   Anyone who knows about fish physiology will know that Malmo's design would suddenly poach the fish to death, some-time-anytime, but definitely before the first year is out. Not in the Chinese style of poached fish, the whole fish, covered with scallions and sliced ginger on a long oval dish, hot oil and soy sauce poured over just before serving. But in the style of dead fish, bloated, opaque eyes, little fins up, doing the back float in a too warm pool of water. Knocking, knocking hello-farewell against a Lucite sky. Adios. [Note to Note #2: *Adiós*, from the Spanish a Dios (*Lat. ad deus*): to God.]

3.   Anyone who knows about heat exchange systems using kitchen waste heat will know how the fish would die. Malmo's thermometer would crash, sometime in the first year, the repeated surge of heat from the hot dishwasher water overtasking Malmo's thermometer. One time, that daily surge of hot dishwater would heat the cabling of the heat exchange system enough to raise the temperature of the water so quickly, the fish would poop, poach, and do the ultimate back float. The bloated corpses bumping against the ultramodern Lucite floor.

4.   Anyone who knows about peculiar North American food style trends of the yet-to-come '70s, such as whipped edible oil products, fruit leather, and green goddess dressing, will foretell that most unusual '70s culinary practice of slathering a whole salmon with store-bought mayonnaise, wrapping the fish in foil and running it through a full dishwasher cycle to cook it. Moist.]

························

The fish don't die.
Conceit saves the koi.

Malmo wants to show the drawings to Phil, a self-confident colleague, who has done both structural and electrical specs. Whose teeth would drive Vee crazy, if he were only Oriental.

"You putting crab and stuff in here?"

"No," Malmo says, regretting the moment he said to Phil, Let me show you something I've been working on, "Koi. They're large fish. Carp."

"But not, like, good for eating?"

"No. I've never heard of anyone eating koi. They're very rare and expensive fish, Phil. You don't eat them, you keep them in a pond. Strictly ornamental."

"Oriental?"

"Ornamental."

"Well, if you can't figure out a way to cut, gut, and eat 'em, you better change your heat exchanger. God, at least the thermometer. You gonna fry those fish, Buddy. Don't you know the variance between the waste heat values of these appliances? It's like... Size Huge, man. Huge."

Malmo repeatedly tries to terminate the conversation, but later, forty-eight minutes later, he is more resolute than ever to have a koi pond, explaining to Phil that, No, it's not some weirdee Chinese thing Malmo has to do to prove his manliness.

Phil opens his hands to Malmo as if to show him how clean they are.

"Why don't you just put a big aquarium in your kitchen, Mal?"

....

Malmo drops the concept of a heat exchange system in his drawings. He substitutes a primary source electric heating system, with a durable thermometer that can withstand millions of cycles and bumps. Malmo specifies that the thermometer be wired to an alarmed thermoelectric monitoring device, and searches relentlessly for the best one. Finally, he sources a device that can detect minute variances in water temperature from a supplier to a commercial freezer manufacturer. Malmo procures second and third opinions from competitor engineering firms, undertakes discreet, no-name consultations with the membership officer of the Professional Engineering Society to find the quintessential electrical engineer.

Wing drops Lizzie and Pen off at the Downtown YWCA on Saturday mornings for swimming lessons. Every week he says the same thing: Pay attention, and don't go off the deep end.

....

banquette
elegant and modern renovation
good taste
koi are rare and expensive
won't smell
makes house more valuable (bank)
?safer than an open pond (?kids)
banquette
won't smell

?gimmees: columns? bed? patio deck?

Malmo unfolds and looks at his prep sheet. In the end, not as hard as he thought it might be. He knew to sell the new kitchen by the banquette, and not with the concept drawings. He turned the key, started, with the banquette, round, in tan leather, just like the Nancy Kwan movie. He pulled away from the curb, coordinating cupboards, copper tile counter backsplash, expensive dado, new appliances. He threatened to stall, when Vee asked Why, why under the kitchen floor. Skidded on a grease spot when he used the word, thermocouple, once too often. Malmo turned into the skid, coasted gently down the hill in neutral, quietly voicing the word, koi, like gold foil, so Vee's mental brake on all things that she calls Chinese In A Bad Way would not be pumped, the brake cable snapping, and both of them careening out of control into the aftermath of a yin-yang slam-bang, No Way Malmo pile-up.

She didn't even bring up the mattress. None of the ?s. Malmo tears up the page, throws half the scraps in the toilet and flushes; the rest, he pockets and will throw out at work.

....

Once: Malmo will apply for and be granted a second mortgage on the house, despite fully disclosing the nature of his renovation project to the bank. The second mortgage will be largely due to the bank's fear of losing the significant ground they feel they've made with the Oriental community, by mailing bank calendars with the Chinese "Good Luck" symbol in December to anyone whose surname sounds even a little bit Oriental, like Lee, Spong, Low, Keen, and inviting customers at the same time of year to help themselves to a basket of what the bank manager calls Jap oranges. Twice: Harold Parker, head of the Biology department at the University of Alberta, will be paid twice: once, monthly, by Malmo for a year, for consulting on filtration, alkaline levels, acclimatization protocols, bottom fill specs, nutrition sourcing, and other details about the actual fish and their maintenance; and again, for decades, as Harold dines out on the story fodder gifted to him during his one-year association with the man who wanted a fish pond under his kitchen floor. Three times: Malmo will ask and ask and finally persuade Kai, the cook at the Osaka restaurant, to give him the name of the guy in Vancouver who has a cousin who lives in Taipei who knows a stevedore in Hong Kong who works for a man whose brother has the most hardy domesticated koi stock in the world. Third time lucky.

....

Mumma won't go to see Malmo and Vee's new pond, the idea of fish being able to swim between her legs, bulbous sideways eyes peering furtively under her skirt, and in the kitchen of all places is Too Much Thank You.

"C'mon, Mumma," Wing says, "Means a lot to Malmo, and to Vee."

Tom runs wild and Jane toddles after him, up and down the aisles, slowing only when they climb the slope where the floor humps in the middle aisle of Wing's store. Mumma brought Tom and Jane downtown to the store on the bus, specifically one bus to the end of the line, and then a transfer to the second bus going downtown on Wednesday afternoon, when the buses operate on an off-peak schedule. Mumma feels noodle hot, and wants to get home before the older girls are home from school. Wing has almost finished checking the supplier invoices against the ledger, nothing he couldn't finish tomorrow.

"There," she says, taking Wing's plastic magnifying sheet off the open ledger and slapping it down on the top edges of his fish tank at the back of the store, "Let's go home." The fish startle from the sound of the plastic sheet hitting against the frame of the tank, but settle quickly, swimming smoothly past the blue plastic scuba diver aerator.

"Mumma, shouldn't we go see Malmo's new pond?"

"Shouldn't we," Mumma repeats as a statement, "I stopped worrying, even thinking about 'shouldn't we', the minute the nurse at the hospital put baby number four in my arms." Mumma thrusts her left hand out, gesturing toward the fish tank, "What do you need me to do? Put this on the floor so you can watch the fish swim by your feet? Honestly."

Wing laughs. "OK, Mumma. Let's going home."

··

Number 57. One Thousand Year Old Eggs

Mumma takes a man-sized Kleenex from Dad's night table drawer, wraps it securely around a Kotex napkin, and slides the bundle into her navy leather going-out bag, almost filling it. That time of the month, the little visitor, her dot, or, Mumma's favourite term of endurance, the capital C, Curse.

Why does capital C, Curse come at the worst time of the month, Mumma wonders. Why doesn't it come when Mumma has nothing better to do than read those books that Sally Faber keeps foisting on her, naughty books with arching body parts and many speeds of breathing.

Oh who am I kidding, Mumma thinks, looking at the pile of unread books, Me, who can't even say that word, that one. Mumma recalls the unbearably long discussion with Lizzie and Pen years ago, talking about bird and bee, Pen keeping

··

at her and at her, even after Lizzie went back to watching *The Forest Rangers* on TV with Tom and Jane, "No, Mumma, it doesn't make sense that if you just lie close together with a man you love, you'll get pregnant. It just doesn't make sense. Why do you have to love them? Do you have to love them? Bet you don't even have to like them. Andy McLaughlin's oldest sister is pregnant and I heard her say she hasn't felt true love in forever and forever. Plus also, I bet you don't even have to lie down. No, I bet you can be standing right up. Straight up, Mumma. You know, I stand up on the bus in rush hour surrounded by people. Strangers. Some of them are men — do you mean to tell me I could get pregnant on the Number 1 Jasper Place coming home in rush hour just because I'm standing up, close to men? Shouldn't there be a law about women and men standing together on the bus, Mumma? Who wants to get pregnant with some stranger-on-the-bus's baby? Something's fishy, Mumma. Something doesn't sound like love." Mumma doesn't know the word, disingenuous, but she does know that her bird and bee conversation with Lizzie and Pen, even just mentally replaying fragments, can still make a line of sweat break out on Mumma's upper lip. Which does not help one little bit, not at this time of the month.

Okay. Dinky-do. Mumma can go that far, can say that word, a red blush flowing from the base of her throat up to her forehead, even now. Years and years ago, when she talked bird and bee with the older girls, gave them the Young Woman booklet from the Kotex company that she had sent away for, Mumma's reddening reminded Lizzie of the Grade 4 science experiment, capillary action makes the red-dyed water travel up the tubes in a stalk of celery. Pressed and pressed by Pen, and seeing

Lizzie's expression transform from happily curious to dumb-founded and moderately anxious, Mumma mumbled, "You know boys. Boys...boys, they have....they are.... They stand up to pee. Different, right? Remember when Tom was a baby, and you watched me change his diaper? Yeah, all boys have, the reason they can stand and pee.... They have a dinky-do. Yes. They do. They all do. Mm-hmm. And that... Yes, that's, you know, it's Involved With — with bird and bee too."

Because Pen already knew from Andy McLaughlin's sister, and Lizzie made the subconscious association with liquid travelling up the tubes of a firm stalk of celery, Mumma's little talk somewhat followed through on its objectives. At least Mumma hoped that Lizzie wouldn't think that she was dying when her little visitor came the second time, Lizzie behind the bathroom door, "Oh, you go on without me to church. I think I'm dying." [Note: all of Mumma's children will go to university. Each of them will take introductory psychology and kill themselves laughing when they study Freud and psychoanalysis and dinky-do envy.]

Mumma's hands press against the sides of her navy going-out purse as if she is holding a closed book between the palms of her hands. Nope. There's just no room for a second pad, a just in case Kotex. Darn it, a sanitary napkin double-indemnity insurance policy just will not fit into Mumma's smart-looking going-out bag. Mumma knows that if you have a second pad, you won't need it. Take an umbrella with you downtown in the Spring, on that day with the bluest sky, so the unforeseen, unforecasted cloudburst won't wet slap you across the back of your head and flatten your curls. Same principle. Mumma craves the security of a spare Kotex, Mumma being accident-free for way more consecutive seasons and years than any construction site registered under the provincial occupational health and safety regime.

Damn capital C, Curse. Mumma opens her smart bag with the solo Kotex inside. Well, there's always vending machine Kotex. Ha, as if Mumma has the faith to rely on a ten-cent vending machine that dispenses capital C, Curse protection. As if Mumma has ever procured a sanitary napkin from one of those metal boxes with a handle and a coin slot, mounted on a public ladies' room wall. Mumma maintains a deep mistrust of coin-operated sanitary napkin dispensers, not based on any personal experience or what she's heard said, as if anyone has ever talked about trying a sanitary napkin vending machine. Mumma does not trust any vending machine, but especially sanitary napkin vending machines.

When it comes to vending machine commerce, Mumma believes the only certain thing is that you certainly won't get what you want. Actually not just want, but need, you will not get what you need when you need it. Mumma knows in her head that women must rely on these machines and find them handy and easy to operate, because they're on the wall in practically every public ladies' room. But Mumma's heart tells her that at the very moment when she desperately needs a ten-cent vending machine Kotex, when she is pressing her knees together and willing every muscle and bone, each fascia, all the cells in her body to stay self-contained, as status quo as possible, against the odds, when that thin silver dime disappears down the slot in the machine and she turns the nickel-plated handle — in her imagination, Mumma sees a stream of hot coffee sweetened with two sugars pouring into the metal tray at the bottom of the machine, then dripping onto the ladies' room floor; or a paper cup dropping down, followed by a thick jet of yellow chicken soup; possibly a defective box of Bridge Mixture tumbling down the chute, open-ended side down, clattering the restroom floor with a shower of shiny brown pellets. Mumma doesn't have the load-bearing capacity to shoulder that much embarrassment. She scowls, imagines herself in a ladies' restroom, with women, tittering, shaking their heads as they watch her, knees cemented together, trying to dislodge a Styro cup full of hot cocoa with hard little white marshmallows out of a Kotex vending machine, when all she wants — no, needs — is a sanitary napkin! Mumma feels the blood rushing up the back of her neck.

She will simply have to change her Kotex right before going out. Okay, Mumma thinks, I'll wear the spare. Knowing this is not a great solution, Mumma shrugs her shoulders, she whispers under her breath, Damn capital C, Curse.

Mumma's a keen troubleshooter, with mad skills for calmly attending to quotidian logistics, budgeting, medium and long range planning. Not exactly a perfectionist but right next door to it, Mumma's miffed by the inelegant and half-baked solution of changing her Kotex right before going out.

Heaven knows, Kotex isn't the problem, having saved the day for moments unrelated to capital C, Curse. Mumma fingers the fasteners on the spare Kotex and recalls how she first came upon using Kotex for a bridal shower gift.

[Note: it will be years from now, during the halcyon days, no, the years dedicated to self-absorption and self-help, when people will talk about "finding their passion," or "doing what you love and you'll never work a day in your life." But if people had the mind-set to declare, even to think about what floated their boats, gave them their goodies, what zip-a-deed their do-dahs, at the time that Mumma was packing her smart going-out purse with the solo Kotex, Mumma would have said, "Oh that's easy. I throw fabulous bridal showers."]

Mumma enjoys a reputation for her creativity when it comes to bridal showers. God knows, Mumma may be an imposter with the Chinese language Bible in the House of the Lord, an ecclesiastical linguistic poseur, but what every woman in the congregation knows is that if your daughter is getting married, blessed be the family that Mumma Lee favours by throwing one of her memorable bridal showers.

God only knows why Mumma's showers have such a devoted following, RSVPs 100% yes, with guests coming early and staying Late, late late. Is it the tiny cream puffs shaped like golden choux pastry swans, the top of the puff sliced in two pieces and fitted like wings into the cream-filled bottom, a slender choux pastry "S" placed to suggest the neck and graceful head of a pastry bird? How about the tomato roses, the pearly white onion mums, the celery dahlias, and the carrot daisies in Mumma's carefully arranged bridal garden vegetable platters? Could it be Mumma's salmon in aspic recipe from Janet Peters's recipe book, Janet Peters, who women in the know kind of knew was actually Norah Willis Michener, noted philosopher, etiquette expert, hostess, home economist, and wife of the Governor General? [Note: God knows it shouldn't be, but...] No, mostly it's the way Mumma decorates the presents she gives to each bride-to-be.

Mumma remembers setting up her own household, knows that every bride could use a little help, a leg up, a hoot boost from behind, in collecting her kitchen linens — two crisp linen tea towels and a good quality dish cloth, the durable kind on which a young bride might not think to splurge her household allowance. Initially, Mumma tucked the kitchen linens into the sides of the box, holding her gift like tissue. Then one afternoon, as she wrapped up a tea cup and saucer, shortly after a Communion Sunday church service, shortly after seeing Dougie spin the linen napkins before dim sum at the New World, spinning linens bringing to mind a beautiful Leslie-Caron-*An-American-in-Paris* style wide-gore (not a Lesley-Gore-*American-Bandstand*-cry-if-you-want-to) party skirt, Mumma's hands began to fiddle. A few finger pleats here and some accordian folding there, a twist there and another one there, a little criss-crossing, and three firm tucks.

"Tah-Dah?" Mumma queried, still not quite certain she could trust her eyes, each syllable having the same emphasis. Her hands held a little headless maiden wearing a long dress with cap sleeves, entirely made from two tea towels, with a dishcloth apron tucked in at the waist. What a wonder, she thought. Mumma frowned at the absence of a head.

But Mumma would never go out and buy a small Styrofoam ball adorned with a wiry pot scrubber wig, or a skein of baby yarn, rolled and braided into a head with a hairdo to finish the doll. Mumma came to decide that her bridal shower maiden doll would have a head with exquisitely drawn-on features but made from a sanitary napkin, rolled and tied by its own fasteners.

Mumma checks her makeup in her compact mirror, and slides the compact in beside the Kotex. Lizzie already in university, early admission. Lizzie brought home a black-and-white booklet on human reproduction printed by the Students' Union, just about the time that Mumma noticed the stains on Tom's bedsheets. "Here," Mumma said, handing him the booklet, "if you want to talk about this, you better ask your father." [Note: Years after Mumma loses track of the Students' Union booklet, when it's Jane's turn for The Talk, Mumma will give Jane the Kotex Young Woman booklet to review beforehand. During Mumma's mumble to Jane, "They lie down very close together, they do. So close — and they think about the baby they would like to have," Mumma's left hand will inscribe the air with an all-encompassing arc which will be twinned by the two black eyebrow arcs over Mumma's you-better-pay-attention eyes. The total effect of Mumma's talk and Jane's pre-reading the booklet will leave Jane convinced that if a man sitting beside her on the Number 1 Jasper Place bus takes off his shoe to scratch the ball of his foot, she will catch a social disease.]

It's Dad who complicates their lives, Mumma thinks. Dad gets tangled in the burrs of other people's lives, and then drags them all in with him. Where most mothers in the neighbourhood worry about their kids bringing home stray kittens and lost dogs, Dad brings home whole families.

Or he goes to them, an endless ledger of honour debts that distant relations, friends of old, paper Uncles, friends of acquaintances always call on Dad to settle. "He knew my father and wanted to be buried in China," Dad says, "His widow doesn't speak any English, doesn't know anyone there who speaks English very well." Dad pocketed the train ticket for Vancouver in the inner pocket of his coat. "We talked about this, it's the right thing to do, God knows, to help someone get to the place where they want to be laid to rest."

Mumma wipes invisible dust from the body of her navy going-out purse using her closed fingers as a dust cloth. What Dad does is right, but what comes out her mouth never talks to her mind first.

"You make it sound like he's still alive," Mumma said as she folded tissue around two white dress shirts and placed the packages into Dad's brown leather suitcase, "Why Wing, why would someone want to be buried in China? Why would they never go back, would they work and raise families and retire here, but be sure that's where they want to be buried?"

"I don't know, Mumma," Dad said.

"What about the store?"

"Store's fine, you know it is. Gee Bahk's son is going to be fine on his own for a couple of days."

"Well, have you thought about just burying him in the Chinese cemetery in Vancouver? I'm sure his widow could use the extra money."

"   "

"Well?"

"You know Mumma, you tell the kids the same thing when they've lost something. You say, 'Where did you see it last? Where did you have it last, and if you retrace where you went from there, you'll find it again.' Who knows what he's looking for, but if he's saying China, I say, 'Sure, why not?'"

Mumma tenses her shoulders, runs the navy purse straps through her hands. Mind is right, still right, she thinks, but something just out of view hides in there, wrapped under layers like a head of cabbage leaves.

When Mumma shut Dad's suitcase, that time packed for Medicine Hat, the snap of brass locks reminded her to try this time to have mouth talk to her mind first.

"I've known them since the Imperial Cafe days, and now Diamond and his brothers have saved enough for a business. They can run a store, I'm pretty sure, but they have no idea what fixtures to buy, how to set up their books, what they need to watch out for, how to bargain," Dad said as they waited at the bus station, the neighbour babysitting the younger kids, one of Dad's feet resting on the brown suitcase, a bus ticket to Medicine Hat in his coat pocket.

"Oh. Yes. Hmmm. Now if you get cold, put on your chamois vest," Mumma said.

"Thanks Mumma," Dad said.

Thanks Mind, Mumma thought, but frowned as she felt something slip to a better hiding place in her mind.

Mumma carefully pats her hair and pokes the tail of her comb here and there to get the curls to stand. Dad travels all over the place. Travel is almost always involved.

"Well, the problem was that they didn't understand that they had to get more pills from the drugstore after the ones from the hospital ran out," Dad explained, dusting the dirt off the back of his pant cuffs as Mumma's hand felt the heat emanating from the hood of the car, "So I took them to the drugstore and the druggist filled the prescription."

"Good for you, Wing," Mumma said, the edge of her lower teeth combing her upper lip gently, as she reached up with her left hand to finger the permy curls under her ear.

....

At home getting ready, Dad wipes the lenses of his binoculars with a soft cloth, and eases the binocs into their leather case. Freddy insists that Wing and Mumma be his and Fairy's guests this afternoon at the track. Dad usually doesn't want anything other than to finish the business, get everything in place and be out, but Freddy insists and Dad loves the ponies. Starting gate, Horses, one chute for every horse, post position, ready, doors open finally all at once, the sound of the bell. Sound and light, Fire connects mind and body, spirit gushes into blood, Spur, crop whips air whips silk, mind and body, Fire connects beast and rider, faster, Mind body mind body, One three two four, muscle bone, faster, Tendons linking muscle bone, faster, faster, Ligaments link bone bone, faster faster, Muscle bone, One body, down the stretch, Pounding, sound light, pounding hoof heart, Faster faster faster.

Photo finish, invisible finish line.

Dad snaps the latch on his binocular case, and takes a man-sized Kleenex from his night table. Wednesday afternoon, the store's closed anyway. Dad loves the ponies.

Dad's not a juicy joyful altruist and he knows it. Rather, Dad fights the weight of what probably will happen if he doesn't help. He's the last chance to steer people clear of disaster, Wing Lee, the reluctant Samaritan. He'd rather be playing tennis, building kites with his son, tending his African Violet collection, or reading African Violet Society journals. But, what about the people on the verge of signing leases they can't read, leases that would have their families, months later, sitting on the front lawn of the place they called home, with their white enamel pots, darned socks, long underwear, flour sack nightshirts, and one or two spare shirts mounded beside them. Or people who can't read prescription labels for themselves or for their children, so Dad improvises a primitive blister pack dispenser with folded tan-coloured kraft paper from the store, paper-clipped around the edges of a piece of cardboard.

Dad also helps with all the translations and arrangements involved in the aftermath of a death in a family. A family grieving a death need not die twice by holding a funeral they can't afford. A financial disaster in the aftermath of a death leaves a rusty metallic taste that lingers on the tongue, so this should be avoided. Like that Vancouver business, "Yes I know these are not very common arrangements anymore," Wing choosing his words carefully, to the reluctant man at the funeral parlour who said that he could not recall the last time that he had to arrange "one of these hincty Chinaman burials." God knows Wing Lee bears up to Gravity in his choice of words most days of the week, believing that his children will not have to choose their words as carefully as he does.

"Ready Mumma?" he calls down the hallway.

....

Turning from the mirror in the bathroom, Mumma catches a whiff of her face powder, a fleeting reminder of life before becoming Mumma. Surely the right thing, helping Freddy and Fairy with their son. Fairy's a good mother, knew enough not to let anyone close the door on the boy. He couldn't go to the neighbourhood school, so how could the brand new School for the Deaf, the publicly-funded school for the deaf, try to bar his admission because English wasn't spoken in the home? That's when Freddy called Dad for help, at Fairy's urging. Fairy, Ng Fei-lan in Chinese, "Fairy," a given name a bureaucrat literally gave her, Fairy was what rubbed the Immigration Officer's whimsy and the tip of his pen, as Fei-lan presented her papers in Victoria, B.C. [Note: Here's a Venn diagram for Immigration Officers back in the day: All of them creative writers, by necessity, assigning names, recording subjective visual assessments; Immigration Officers (A) and Creative Writers (B); A, a small circle entirely inside and hugging the arc of the much larger circle, B. However, only a few Immigration Officers also belonged in the circle Compassionate Humanists (c) when creating Anglophone names for certain newcomers; those few used (the rest, abused) the discretion given to them in the policy directive to create a homophone of the Applicant's name in the applicable mother tongue; the union of circle A and C a very small intersection. Ask any of the many naturalized citizens and landed immigrants whose given names mimic children's storybook or cartoon character names, not of the King or princess but more of the dog, duck and cow subgenre.] [Note to previous Note: How big should you draw Circle C? — draw it wide.]

Dad always does the right thing, no doubt Dad does good things for lots of families, but with so many people, Dad is spread as thin as the skin of a soap bubble. And here we are, Mumma shakes her head at the thought, going to the racetrack in the afternoon with Freddy and Fairy when I've got the capital C, Curse.

Ohhh. Mumma feels the hot slippery wet leave her body. Damn capital C, Curse, oh please God, no accidents today.

....

Yesterday, Tom stayed home, sick, so this morning, he needed a note. Grabbing the first pen out of the Fry's Cocoa tin, Mumma scribed a quick note.

"Mumma, I can't take this to school," Tom looked at her, his chin tucked under indignant eyes, "You've written it in red pen. Red ink, Mumma. Don't you get it? Everyone will think you're a Communist. Everyone will think we're all Communists."

Mumma's little visitor had just come that morning, day one, first is the worst. "Oh give it here then," she said to Tom, scribbled on the note, and handed it back.

Under her signature, Mumma had written in faint red letters, "The Communist." She volleyed Tom's I-mean-business eyes right back into his court, and he turned away when he couldn't volley back. He folded the note in quarters and tucked it into the pages of his Speller.

"Ready as I'll ever be," Mumma calls back to Dad.

What a combination, Mumma thinks, the track and capital C, Curse. In her mind, Mumma pictures the sweat-glistening flanks of bay thoroughbreds pounding the metal out of their shoes, four hooves in rhythm, the counterpoint dance of the field of eight horses, drumming the track, their sticky black manes and tails whipping the air. At least the racing program details what's happening and will happen next; a clear starting point and an equally clear finish line; and only one route, only one direction the race can go. Mumma feels the hotpot-steamy bundle between her legs and thinks the track may be the perfect place to go. The kids are all in school and can take care of themselves once they get home.

·················

Jane sits in her wooden desk and inhales Grade 1: the lead and wood shavings smell of chubby yellow HB pencils with the lousy hard erasers that rub holes in practice books; the good pink erasers, dangling from a long white string tied to the arm of each student's desk; the heady smell of the amber mucilage bottles topped with a red rubber nipple, the small slash opening on the flat angular side of the nipple gaping like a tiny red mouth under Jane's fingers; the perfume of mimeographed pages fresh from the Gestetner machine; the earthy suffusion of clayish-wet poster paint thickly applied to pulpy manila paper. Jane raises her hands and cups her nose to capture the super-duper Grade 1 aroma.

Grade 1 presents a visual feast for Jane too, a gallery of autumn leaves ironed between two pieces of wax paper and hung like laundry in two diagonal lines from each corner of the room; gold foil stars; unbroken series of red-pencil check marks, check, and check, and check; a large poster of a hair comb, a toothbrush, and a drawing of clean, unbitten fingernails attached to a washed hand, with a graph tracking the daily personal hygiene assessments for each child; and of course Nicky Staples's bum-bum. Nicky Staples has the pinkest, roundest bum-bum, an exquisite, non-replicable shade of pink, in any medium, be it flesh or flower, tint or dye, eraser or bubblegum. She only sees Nicky's bum-bum once ever, when Nicky, finished his work, stood quietly beside his desk and easing his hands into the elastic waistband of his husky boy pants, pulled the back of his pants down to scratch his bare buttocks, just at the moment when Jane looked over her shoulder two desks behind her.

For Jane, every day of Grade 1 is the wildest dream come to life, Grade 1 is dessert after every meal, riding on a parade float, an unending supply of grape Life Savers. Some days, you learn how to lay your coat on the floor, upside down, stand by the collar, bend your knees, put your hands inside the armholes, then swing that coat over your head to leave for recess and for home. Some days, you watch a film on safety near train tracks and rail yards, and even though you've never seen a train except from Dad's car and you live twenty-seven miles from the nearest train tracks, for sure, you will never play in or near an open box car. Some days, you practice hiding under your desk when Mrs. Shaw blows her whistle and Gregory Bailey falls asleep, again, because his mumma gives him little bits of her calm pills. Some days, Muriel Dubbick's father and another man come to school and give each child a soft, burgundy leather Bible, and Jane calls it her Dale Evans Bible because Mr. Dubbick and his friend say the Bible is from the Giddyups.

But then Muriel Dubbick teaches you how to make angel hair and nothing prepares you for angel hair.

Who knew? Who knew that the amber-coloured glue in the bottle with the red rubber nipple, [Note: Grade 1 Jane calls this a dauber or red thing. She knows but in Grade 1 never says the word, nipple, could never have called a nipple a nipple, after all, she is her Mumma's daughter.] who knew that amber glue, when rubbed between a thumb and pointer finger, then pinching and opening, pinching and opening those fingers around the pointer finger of the other hand would spin a tiny muff of white iridescent floss. Muriel slipped the glue bottle into her jacket pocket after she threw her jacket over her head at the start of recess bell. On the tarmac, the white cocoon grows more fragile-looking and yet lush on the creator's pointer finger, with each pass of Muriel's finger loom.

"See? Angel hair," Muriel declares.

Connecting Muriel's act of creation and confident declaration with Mr. Dubbick's role as deliverer of Dale Evans Bibles, Jane sees Muriel's angel hair literally. Maybe, this is part of what goes on at church, once a month. Maybe, if Jane went to church where people spoke English, angel hair would not come as such a surprise. Angel hair. Until this very day, Jane never had the notion of starting with English words to be translated into Chinese. Maybe, she thinks, maybe I am getting closer to understanding about church and House of the Lord. Jane hears Dad tell her to "make a mental note like Mumma does" to remember to ask Mumma how to say angel hair in Chinese, then Jane adds a note to the note to listen for angel hair, whatever angel hair sounds like in Chinese, in the minister's sermons, but there's a hole in the pocket of her mental jacket where she stuffs the note, and when she throws that jacket over her head to leave for home, the note gets permanently lost in the mental lining.

"Can I see?" Jane asks.

"Sure," Muriel says, "You can even hold it." Muriel touches the tip of her pointer finger to Jane's and uses the third and ring finger of her other hand like a fork with two tines, transferring a delicate morsel from one shish kabob skewer to another.

Jane feels the coolness of Muriel's fingertip as the white angel hair moves down Muriel's tiny digit. Jane swallows, and feels the greasy armpit, sticky palm feeling she gets when Mumma says Jane's becoming over-ragitated. As the circle of angel hair moves onto Jane's finger, it hugs her finger in a snug feeling, but very quickly, Jane feels the angel hair hug slacken. The angel hair begins to dissolve from around Jane's finger.

"You're too hot. Look at your finger, it's melting," Muriel complains, "Give it back, give it back before it all disappears."

Jane wants nothing more than to have the angel hair restored intact on Muriel's cool white finger. However, the disappearing angel hair has become trapped by a sticky crust of amber-coloured glue on Jane's pointer finger, and when Jane tries to imitate Muriel's finger fork with her other hand, the angel hair sticks to those fingers, and melts completely, covering Jane's fingers with sticky, amber crusts.

"I'm sorry, Muriel. I'm really really sorry."

"Well, I guess it's not your fault. I mean, not really," Muriel says, shaking her head, "I suppose it's not something that just anyone can do, spin angel hair. Seems like some people can't even hold it. Your fingers are just too hot," she concludes, the end of recess bell sounds to confirm her findings.

Jane looks at her dirty sticky fingers, more amber brown than usual. Jane feels her heart pressing against the muscles of her chest wall, feels the same dead eye feeling she felt when they were reading aloud in class and Muriel raised her hand and said, "I think Jane in *Dick and Jane* looks more like a real girl named Jane, than Jane Lee looks like a real Jane," and everyone laughed, until Mrs. Shaw shushed them. Jane tries following Dad's advice from a while ago, before starting playschool, to "think and be positive, that's what Father Brady would say," then, slumping her shoulders, Jane realizes, of course, the good Father would never have any problems with angel hair. Jane mimics the motions of Muriel's finger loom, but Jane's shuttles are lousy with brown sticky crusts.

Jane balls both hands as she stands by the line of brass coat hooks at the back of the classroom and shrugs her coat off her shoulders. She picks up the cord hanging-loop sewn in the collar of her jacket with a clean pinky finger and hooks the loop over an empty hook in the middle of the row. Carefully, she smooths her coat into the wedge of space left between the two adjacent coats with the back of her wrist.

"Jane Lee, what's that on your hands?" Mrs. Shaw asks.

Angel hair, Jane wants to say, yes, hair of the very angels that she has heard on high. Oh yes, all the time, Jane imagines declaring to Mrs. Shaw, Yes, and they have white wings that bend near the earth, so close, they are really only a hand's grasp away, angels with beautiful white angel hair.

"School glue, Mrs. Shaw."

"Well. I know a young lady who should go down to the girls' washroom and wash her hands lickety-split so she doesn't lose today's check mark and the whole week's treat for having dirty hands. Do you know who that would be? I think it's the same young lady who knows better than to play with glue."

"Yes, Mrs. Shaw."

School soap from the silver dispenser mounted on the wall in the girls' washroom makes lots of bubbles, but stings and smells like the janitor's sink where you pour leftover paint. Jane runs home at lunch and after school rather than use the girls' washroom at school, hard black toilet seats and bad soap. But Jane needs the soap to keep today's checkmark, her perfect row of checkmarks. When Jane brings home the mimeograph sheet of one hundred addition questions, one hundred miniature equation boxes at perfectly spaced intervals, ten across and ten rows, she has red pencil [Note: Laurentian #3 Poppy

Red, or possibly Dixon Ticonderoga Teacher's Marker #425T Carmine Red, because, No, Mrs. Shaw would not use, would not even know how to access Communist Red, perish the thought.] checkmarks against ninety-six of the boxes, and a "96" standing on a horizontal line above "100," an unreduced fraction written at the top of the page.

"Where are the four you missed?" Dad asks.

"I got ninety-six right. I just didn't get four of them," Jane says.

"Yes I know. If you work hard the next time, you won't miss those four. If you work hard, you will do well."

"You mean everything will be right?"

"I mean nothing will be wrong," Dad says.

Jane scours her amber brown hands and palms with the tops of her fingernails, and as the smell of bad soap scrapes its way around the bowls of Jane's nostrils, the few strands of white angel hair spinning down from her fingers dissolve under running water.

....

Although not in these words, Mumma believes that the worst form of self-debasement is afternoon television soap opera. Soaps are worse than garbage. However, one of the local stations runs a movie, every weekday right after lunch, during a program slot called *Siesta Cinema*, and every once in a while, on Tuesdays and every other Thursday, Mumma sets the ironing board up in front of the television and turns it on for background noise. So, it comes as no surprise that every time Mumma sits in the passenger seat going down the driveway, on her mental screen, there's a close-up of Leslie Howard, or Cary Grant, or

Michael Caine, saying to her, "Don't look back Mumma," but darn if she always does anyway.

She can't help it. Everything about home makes sense: home gets dirty, clean it up; home gets empty, fill it up; home get wobbly, straighten it up. But every step away from home deepens the pool of the acid low down in Mumma's throat. The world has infinite bodies that orbit around home, and every orbit farther away from home is steeped in What If/Oh No, then: Get a grip/No Way.

....

Communist, "Oooah," *kick*.
Communist? "Mmmmmh," *kick*.
Red Communist, "Uhhhhh," *kick*.

Tom tries to smooth the wrinkles out of the fabric of his world when he kicks the tetherball on the school playground. At morning and afternoon recess, coming back early after lunch, and for hours after school, Tom Lee kicks the tetherball. The ball flies into the air, the curve prescribed by the force of Tom's leg muscles and the length of the tether, then mid-air, the ball is pulled up short, jerked back. The ball convulses, then moves in quickly for a closer look at gravity. Closer, come closer, Gravity whispers. Before anything more meaningful gets going between Motion and Gravity, the tetherball is sent flying by the next kick, perfectly timed and landed, Tom Lee, the physical physicist.

Mumma, "Uhfffff," *kick*.
Couldn't be, "Puhhhh," *kick*.
Born in Calgary, "Mhmmm," *kick*.
Shops too much, "Haaaaaa," *kick*.
Dad, "Huwhhhh," *kick*.

Too busy, "Huwhhhhh," *kick*.
Too small, "Yuhhhhh," *kick*.
Red ink, "Hauhhhh," *kick*.
Still, "Yhaaaaaa," *kick*.
Lemon juice, "Uhaaaa," *kick*.
Candle heat, "Wuhhh," *kick*.
Invisible ink, "Puhhh," *kick*.
Wish, "Ahhh," *kick*, "Ahhh," *kick*, "Ahhh," *kick*.

[Note: In only a few years from now, Bruce Lee and kung-fu and martial arts flow into mainstream North American culture, and when they do, the kids who go to school with Tom Lee will remember him as that oriental kid, whose dad taught him karate and all the martial arts at home in their basement and he was always practising in the schoolyard and, they'll say, he was trained and super talented; scared the shit out of them because he could really send that tetherball flying with just his feet, and that could have been somebody's head. In fact, the Lee family's basement overflows with Dad's African Violets, there is no room for kung-fu mats and costume wardrobes, or a secret chamber for throwing stars, death sticks and other martial arts paraphernalia, no room except for yet one more African Violet, from time to time. Dad will not teach Tom how to kill a man with two fingers, but how to dip his soup spoon at the edge of the bowl for manners, and because soup is cooler there than right in the middle, Don't get burned Son, Dad will say. When Tom first goes to see Bruce Lee in *Fists of Fury*, he's grateful that he passed through his grades in a charmed time capsule, never challenged by someone's big brother, or a new kid from Onoway or Saskatoon or some such exotic location, to see "just how tough he really was" because Tom knew how tough he really wasn't. But because they left him alone, he lived only in dread of someone stopping him, the mythic kung-fu boy-master, from hogging the tetherball.] [Note to the previous note: The other specific thing Dad will teach only Tom is how to urinate standing up. Mumma will say, "I can do everything else, I've taught these kids Everything, but I don't have, you know, I do not have, well, I don't have — The Time, the time to teach him that."

"Son," Dad will say to Tom, who will stand in front of the toilet on a low wooden step that Dad builds for this purpose, "You're not eating soup. Don't aim for the edge of the bowl, you'll make a mess. A gentleman aims right in the middle."

"Like this, Dad?"

"Watch what you're doing!"

Dad will shake his head, and use his right hand to turn the top of Tom's head like a spigot, back to what he's doing so Tom will learn to aim like a gentleman.

And Dad will teach Tom how to make a kite out of a pink dry cleaning bag and bamboo plant stakes that goes higher than any of the fuhcockta rainbow, mylar streamer-ed, polka-freckled pretenders that Tom buys for his own son years later, because Tom really doesn't know how to make a kite out of a dry cleaning bag and bamboo plant stakes, wasn't really paying attention when Dad was teaching him, didn't actually hear Dad saying, as he lay the bamboo kite frame on top of the pink dry cleaning bag, "Father Brady says, 'Waste not want not'," was red-cheek mortified going out to the park with his home-made Paramount Cleaners dry cleaning bag kite, until every kid wanted one of Mr. Lee's high-flying pink dry cleaning bag kites.]

....

It's a noisy crowd in the stands at Northlands racetrack. Mumma likes Fairy well enough, sitting beside her in the grandstand seating, with Wing and Freddy sitting together in the row right in front of the ladies. Mumma can't picture them going grocery shopping together, or having coffee in the afternoon. But, to her credit, Fairy is charming and quiet, and doesn't give Mumma that vibe that many women from China give her: so you were born here, that makes everything easier for you in this country, but I am still superior to you in every single way that matters.

Cigarette smoke rings Fairy and Mumma, the Daily Double being both an option for bettors, and the addictive personality pairing of racetrack gambling and smoking. Wing and Freddy both smoke, indeed, very few people at the track do not smoke, other than Mumma and Fairy.

Mumma doesn't mind the smell as much as the baffling notion of so many people in one place who don't mind having little sticks of fire so close to their eyeballs and brains. No, don't think about that Mumma, she says to herself, as she sends a neural memo down to her pelvic floor to behave — so far, so good. She and Fairy share a Racing Form, and they agree that they don't need to spend one cent of their household allowances to have fun at the track.

....

Pen funnels smoke from her lower lip upward, a funnel cloud starting at lip level and spiralling up, as she slouches against the loading dock wall behind the school. Pen's one open eye on the smoke cloud sends a message along her optic nerve that tells her brain how cool she looks. That's what they do after drama club, hang out at The Crate, so named for the abandoned palettes stacked on the west end of the metre-high loading dock to create a rough wooden divan and a palette ottoman.

For Pen, drama club has become her detested salvation, as it has for every member of the club. United by a passionate desire for Voice and Connection, club members are also joined by their antipathy to expose and palpate Neediness, bear witness to Vulnerability, all of it so highly visible in the mirrors of each other. The Crate makes a natural stage for drama club members, and the current governance model is a democracy, everyone in drama club having an opportunity to take a turn holding Court from the stage of the Crate, while the encouraging audience stands on the asphalt pad below.

Pen stubs her cigarette on the loading dock wall and flicks the butt stage left, right off the edge of the loading dock onto the asphalt pad. Pen has always been the Supreme Ruler of Improv, most recently, improvising for herself a fold along the length of her eyelid where one does not exist, so she can apply Mary Quant eye shadow and jet-black pencil liner, exactly as the photos in *Seventeen* and *Glamour* and *Miss Chatelaine* magazines instruct, the eyelid fold being forefront in all the Make Up Tips for Beautiful (read, the Good) Eyes. The requisite creativity and imagination for improv comes naturally to Pen, pinching her nose in front of the bathroom mirror at home to imagine what elongated nostrils would look like, draining as much sauce and garlic and onion from Chinese food to blend herself molecularly with her contemporaries.

Pen walks to the front of the stage, thrusts her arms out, a victorious Eva Peron from the palace balcony, and waits until she has drawn every speck of attention from the audience.

The palette chair and ottoman of The Crate have never looked more like a throne. Then she waits just one beat longer, her victorious, mesmerizing eyes bearing down on them, her smile replicating itself in each mirror she sees standing on the asphalt. "Catch me," she shouts.

....

Lizzie hurries south in the direction of Chinatown, first time in her life in this part of the city not on a Sunday, walking back from the McTeague Co-op. The Co-op houses a collaboration of social workers, psychologists, law students, retired nurses, and volunteers who help the last and the least in East downtown Edmonton, patching the patches on leaks in the inner tube of humanness. Not old enough to legally drink, but old enough to think she knows what she wants, Lizzie, the fresh-faced new volunteer, now, is not so sure social work is what she thought it was, Lizzie, the first year Arts student.

Dad makes it look so easy, helping people. "On the paper slip, I write what the product is and a description of the picture on the label, in Chinese, and also the English name. Then I wrap the paper around the can, and keep it in place with an elastic band, most of the company label still shows, corn starch, baking powder, Ajax cleanser. I write directly on boxes, use a black pencil for food, and a red one for warning, for soaps and cleaning products. When something runs out, people can take the can labels or those paper slips with them to the store, or cut out the boxes if they're not sure, and either put the paper slips I've made back on the new cans, or write the words on the new boxes themselves. One or two times, then they just throw out the slips, or show someone else how to use them, doesn't take long for people to figure out what's what. Most canned food has a picture of the food on the label, people pick that up fast, no need to tag. And fresh is what it looks like too. Makes a big difference for someone who can't read English, and not much work at all, just a bag of elastic bands, red and black grease pencils and slips cut from brown paper. Easy.

"Sometimes," Dad says, "simple as giving someone an alarm clock so their kids get up in time for school, gets the whole family on a daytime schedule, not the whole family on one person's graveyard schedule. Or you take someone shopping, for clothing, or a bed, they have money but don't know how the store works. Sometimes you just make sure people are treated right, no one should have to overpay just because they don't understand, or think they have to buy something where they're being treated badly. Or you just listen so they know someone hears them.

"Basically Lizzie," Dad concludes, "you only know you've really grown up when you know whether, when, and how to take care of other people and you follow through, like tennis. Helping people, like tennis, takes practice. Ball only goes where you want it to go effectively and without injuring yourself when you follow through on the shot. And you only get better, like tennis, the more you practice with people who can improve your game."

She loves the stories Dad tells, in which common sense and ingenuity seem to easily and quickly fix people's problems. But the man she met for an intake interview this afternoon who came to talk about a problem with his roommate wasn't just talking about the roommate at all. Listening to all the twists and rips in his life story, where a car accident which was not his fault, led to chronic back pain, nothing compared with his even now more depressed mother and her amputated feet, a girlfriend who was killed, a stillborn baby, being conned and totally set up by a prodigal brother he located for his mother, a stint in Bowden that came with a Hep B infection, if he hadn't got so sick, he would never have gone back to that apartment block and taken on an unstable roommate who isn't paying his share of the rent but is dealing drugs out of their unit, and he'd just walk away if he had the funds from a big lawsuit settlement that was stolen from his mother, one misfortune after another linked back into all the prior ones, for Lizzie, the afternoon was like a crying magician pulling an endless handkerchief out of his mouth, a long thin cloth that gets rustier, grittier, and more bloody with each yank until you finally realize that he is pulling out his entire viscera. So you want to tell him stop, you don't know how to fix that, you didn't even know that could happen.

"I've taken very detailed notes, and my supervisor will review your case, and if you fit within the guidelines, you will be assigned a caseworker to help you," Lizzie says, diligently following her volunteer training, "Someone will be in touch within two to five business days."

As she put on her coat to leave, she heard the volunteer coordinator and one of the counselors talk about how they were going to approach the local drugstore owner who still sells men's aftershave to some of their clients, men who are not buying a bottle a day to keep their newly shaved faces feeling fresh and rash free.

"What do they buy it for?" Lizzie asked.

Madge, the volunteer coordinator, said, "It's almost pure alcohol, Hon, makes people very, very sick."

"Oh."

"We seeing you again, next week, Lizzie?"

Madge wished she had a nickel for every time one of these younger and younger students says to her, "We'll see." If she did, she'd have three paid caseworkers for every one of their clients and a storefront open 24 hours a day. Still and all, you have to keep trying with these kids, you never know when one of them will stick.

....

Beautiful Dancer, Come to Papa, Prattlin' Madeline, Blue Hawaii, Mumma loves the names they give these thorough-bred race horses, names like pithy songs that are over and done in the time it takes to say them. She and Fairy are up two dollars and sixteen cents in pretend betting over three races. Their heads leaning close to each other over the racing form, they make exceedingly conservative wagers, not wanting to be foolhardy with even pretend money, and keep track of their fake winnings on the racing form. Makes the tote board after each race slightly more interesting than round light bulbs just putting up numbers, and they have decided that they will each spend the full amount of whatever they pretend win on weekend treats for their children.

Mumma roots in her purse for the couple of sticks of spearmint gum she slid into her purse, because a whole package of gum was too bulky. The announcer calls out Post Time for the fourth race on the PA system, catching Mumma's ear. Nine races on the card Wednesdays, so we're not even half the way through the afternoon. As Mumma checks the post time for the fifth race on the racing form, the capital C, Curse math flows through her mind: wonder if I'll make it until after the fifth race before I have to change my pad. Mumma looks at her Kleenex-wrapped Kotex, inhales deeply and slowly breathes out. Where is that gum?

"Are you having fun?" Freddy turns his head around and smiles at Mumma. Dad turns around too.

"Oh yes, thank you, Freddy, and Fairy," she says, turning to her seatmate. "And thank you again for the hot dog," Mumma says, suppressing a small smoky burp. "Are you men having a winning day?" she asks.

"Mhmmm," says Dad, thinking how can Mumma not know you never ask how someone's doing until after the last race on the card, if even then.

Oh, he must be losing, Mumma thinks — he works so hard, she knows that, but she does too, and the kids do too, so why should he spend any time and money on horse racing, gambling, he, the father of four, well, Oh wow. Oh wow is what Mumma says when something has to be said, but words won't do the job. A familiar refrain bubbles up in Mumma's head, kids are fine, their lives so uncomplicated, it's Dad who complicates their lives, and here I am, Wednesday afternoon at the track with this damn capital C, Curse.

....

With two hands, Jane holds the little index card that Mrs. Shaw has put on her desk, there's one on each child's desk when she comes back from the girls' washroom. It has her name typed on it, and Mrs. Shaw says that each child must fill in the correct letter for them on the line beside their name. There are two choices, C or P, and you must fill in which initial represents your

Religion. Mrs. Shaw slowly and loudly informs her pupils that she cannot tell them what the initials stand for, that the children ought to know, based on the house of worship that they attend, that they know the alphabet and they know where they go to Worship, so please fill in the card and put up your hand when you have finished, and then one child will take them to the office. [Note: If this seems unbelievable to you, ask a retired public school teacher if they think this could have happened in the 1960s, the 1970s, last Tuesday. Ask them, then please take them out for dinner.]

Jane's classmates all fill out the cards, and hands go up all over the room. Mrs. Shaw moves between the rows of desks, retrieving the cards. Muriel Dubbick has her hand up, and leans forward, whispering to Amy Taylor, in the desk in front of her, and they both turn to Jane and give her what Jane calls mean smiles.

"Jane Lee," Mrs. Shaw stands beside Jane's desk. "Hurry, please. You're the last one to finish." Jane smells the school soap on her hands. If she only understood more of what went on at church, besides knowing House of the Lord, she is certain she could fill out the card. Then, Jane has a school soap angel hair epiphany. Jane places the card on her desk, turns her head downward and thinks, Oh, I get it now. In her mind, the ladies at church are pinching her cheeks, talking to Mumma. She takes her pencil out of the rounded slot at the top of her desk, looks at her fingers that for the briefest of moments actually touched angel hair, takes a long deep breath and as she exhales, writes "C" for Chinese, (P is for People), certain that she will never be so close to angel hair again in her life.

"An unexcused absence will go on your permanent record, Tom. That would be a shame, but with the Incident last school year, I have no choice, and one more visit to the office will result in an automatic letter to your parents *and* the School Board."

The Incident involved boys at recess running behind, then hooking their hands onto the chrome back bumpers of cars passing in the school zone and seeing how long they could ice ski on the worn treads of their winter boots (prairie winter's equivalent of waterskiing) behind the cars on the icy roads. Principal Howe's letter identified the danger to the children and complaints from concerned motorists, but what really terrified the Lees was that mark on Tom's permanent record. Last school year, what started as an ice capade for Tom, became for Wing and Mumma, a glare ice capastrophe.

"Permanent record," Dad said in Chinese, his hand gripping the letter, after dinner the night that Tom brought the letter home, "Mumma, what does this mean? Does this mean Juvenile Record? Does My Son have some kind of Juvenile Record now? Were the police involved? There were cars. Does this mean no higher education? No university will have him? No university degree, or career? No professional career? Permanent record, is that criminal?"

"No, that can't be" Mumma replied in Chinese, "I... I don't know. I'll talk to the principal. I'll find out, and fix this. Oh wow."

"You're sure you don't have an excuse note?" Principal Howe asks, sitting on the command side of his desk, the tips of his right hand fingers doing push-ups against the tips of his left hand fingers.

Tom feels the folded paper in his pocket, staining the drab white pocket lining with its revolutionary red ink. His hands stay still at his side. "No, sir."

"Shall I Call Your Mother? Ask *her* why you don't have a note to explain your absence?" [Note: Principal Howe does not pull out the big gun lightly, the big gun about calling home, which in less than a decade will look as threatening in a public school principal's office as a bouquet of sweet peas. But this day, the threat of a school communication to a pupil's home that isn't a report card or a permission slip for the annual school trip to the water treatment plant usually breaks the kid's lie wide open.]

"She's not home, Principal Howe."

"Oh, she's not?"

"No. She's at the racetrack, with my dad. He's not working, so they went to the racetrack. With friends."

"Oh," Principal Howe says, (Wednesday at the ponies!) a little irritated since the kid doesn't appear to be lying at all. Howe drums his desk blotter with his fingertips, feels edgy because something or other keeps knocking at the door of his conscience, nudging him to admit he was not terribly interested in why the kid didn't produce an excuse note in the first place. "Permanent record then, Tom?"

"OK."

Later, Principal Howe thinks, I guess I'll be in touch with the Lees anyway. Their youngest was baptized a Catholic. Maybe all the kids? Strange that didn't come up with the older ones, or even Tom. He dictates a letter inviting Mr. and Mrs. Lee to consider a Catholic education for their children, but assuring them that Jane and Tom may remain at his school if the family chooses.

....

Unfolding on the west side of the loading dock behind the high school, a maniacal call-and-response between Pen and her audience. She questions their commitment, and, adoring acolytes, they respond.

"We'll catch you," someone in the crowd calls out.

"Catch me?" she asks, smiling, beseeching, her arms still extended towards them as she steps slightly to her left.

"We Will Catch You," the crowd cries out, moves to their right, every pair of arms outstretched, mirroring Pen's.

"Can I trust you?" Pen howls, doles out being vulnerable and yet still potent and in control.

"Of course! Yeah! Trust us! We will catch you!" Voices pop up all over the audience, and confidently speak for the crowd.

"Are you ready?"

"Yes!" the enthralled audience raises their arms and voices together, all hands cupped to catch Pen.

"Not yet. I can't." The barely perceptible break in Pen's voice suggests an innate knowledge of the social science of charisma, an instinctive understanding that this microscopic faltering will cultivate an even higher degree of identification, of emotional investment by the audience. Pen sways on her feet and the audience sways with her. Pen twists her arms upward as she displays her outstretched hands to the audience. Their arms stretch to come closer, readying themselves to receive.

"Trust us. Jump. C'mon, Pen." The voices of the more vocal acolytes loudly break through the audience, encouraging their leader. Intensity ratchets up one, then another notch.

"Will You Catch Me?" Pen cries, feels as if she conducts pure energy through her limbs.

"We Will Catch You."

"Catch Me," Pen screams, chopping the air with her hands, one time for each word, completely enveloping the drama club in her drama.

Arms reaching skyward, the crowd screams ecstatically in unison voice, "Jummm-puh!"

Pen sprints away from the audience, running east down the entire length of the loading dock, and launches herself hard, pushing her feet off the edge of dock and into a jumble of semi-collapsed cardboard boxes left for burning beside the dumpster. Stunned silence, two seconds, three, when someone starts slow clapping. The audience erupts in screams and applause. The late afternoon sun arrives to bathe The Crate and the audience gathered at the west end of the loading dock. Out of the pool of light, Pen lies still in shadow, her back to The Crate. Underneath her, pain radiates her left arm.

....

By the time she can see the bear on top of the pawnshop in Chinatown, Lizzie is pretty sure that she won't be going back to the McTeague Co-op. With every city block she walked south, she has lost track of more and more details from the intake interview, why did he return to the same apartment block from six years ago, and who was Eugene? As she walks along the sidewalk towards Chinatown, she feels as if she just completed a final exam, and begins to let her mind dump all the cramming, the chronology of events, the different people moving in and out of different segments of the long nylon filament of the man's story.

Feeling ashamed of this shedding, and confused by her nascent indifference to a real person's suffering, a person in need, Lizzie does not understand that she is not the first fish in the world to release herself from a barbless hook. The only details her memory allows her to keep are the shape of the hook, problem with a roommate; the fact that the man wore brown polyester pants carefully tucked into the tops of his cowboy boots; and in the course of their entire time together, instead of using the battered metal ashtray on the desk, for his ashtray, the man used the cowboy boot jiggling on top of his crossed legs, tapping the cigarette on the rim of his boot when the ash grew too long, and popping the filters in when the ash had completely switched places with the tobacco.

Lizzie passes the Foon Key Bean Cake Company sign in front of the grey stucco house, looking as empty today as it does on Sundays. She'll take that story home to family dinner tonight. Two cars hunch together between three diagonal parking lines at the south end of The Coffee Cup Inn's saucer. A third car with a sun-damaged hood and a coat hanger aerial leans on the saucer lot beside the front door. Beside the Coffee Cup Inn's handle, a round pool of urine dampens the dusty lot.

Lizzie stands across the street from the blue-sided pawnshop now, spies the bear on top, his matted fur. She says Hello in her mind, like running into an old friend you might expect to see in a familiar place. As she crosses the street, Lizzie notices something blue near the sidewalk beside the pawnshop. An unsliced loaf of white bread has been roughly broken open lengthwise, and running the length of the loaf is a brilliant turquoise blue stain. Standing now beside the bread, Lizzie can smell a yeasty aftershave smell. The bread has been lodged against the foundation of the pawnshop. [Note: Some clients of The McTeague Co-op pour blue aftershave through whole loaves of white bread to mute the odorants of the aftershave. Do they believe that what comes through the bread is safe to drink? Do they believe that the scent is what makes them sick, not the surrogate alcohol? Do they believe the bread is just a way to make this lethal alcohol bearable to consume because it truly does stink? Asking the bear won't help. Although he's right there, he never sees anything.]

Lizzie can hear the mah jong tiles being washed, the sound of one man speaking Chinese comes out the little window on the side of the pawnshop. Startled, she cranes her neck, but at this angle cannot see the bear. Lizzie frowns, because the bear is hidden to her but in plain view. Lizzie nudges the broken loaf of bread with the large blue stain with her toe, wonders what happens to all the ashes in the man's cowboy boot, not just from today, but ashes collected over all the man's other days strung along the long filament to which those days belong. Blue loaves of bread and cowboy boots full of cigarette ashes. And no foon-kee bear.

....

Mumma's watch and the tote board inform her that Post time for the fourth race is about five minutes away. In Mumma's opinion, this is the best part of the race, before all the drama, before the sorting of those poor horses and jockeys into winners and losers, the kind of thinking in which a pretend bettor can indulge. The eight horses with jockeys on their backs saunter clockwise onto the track. A few of the horses are accompanied by riders on horses, plainly dressed pony boys to keep the horses calm. Some of the horses are accompanied by walking grooms to keep them calm before the race. Track officials on horseback flank the entire post parade to help keep order, and the racehorses calm. To Mumma, it seems the most unhurried, relaxed stroll in the opposite direction that the race will be run, and she loves that, the casual calmness of watching the parade of bi-coloured silks that the jockeys wear, pink and white, turquoise and yellow, royal blue and emerald green, every colour combination her new favourite.

Wing and Freddy return to their seats from the tellers' cages, a few wager tickets in each hand. Fairy and Mumma, both enjoying their chewing gum, send quick little waves with their hands, and when the men have re-settled in their seats in front of them, Fairy and Mumma turn towards each other raising their respective eyebrows.

The horses have arrived at the starting gate, and are being guided by their jockeys and the track employees into their post positions at the gate, each post position separated by open dividers. It suddenly occurs to Mumma that the starting gate is just like getting her kids ready for school in the morning, before she releases them into the world, they run the track, and return home, Mumma the kids' track official. One of the horses balks, refuses to get into its gate. Mumma peels her finger down the program for Race 4, wanting to identify the naughty horse. Just as the announcer calls out the two minutes to post time warning, Mumma's pelvic floor sends up a query, wondering just exactly how soon Mumma will stand up for the first time this afternoon and excuse herself to pay some attention to her southern region. The internal memo flies back down immediately, After this race, don't get your knickers in a knot.

Freddy and Wing arrange and re-arrange their bets, each holding the tickets like a hand of cards. Freddy hopes he wins this time, at least get his money back from placing all these bets on the fourth race. So many bets. He inhales deeply, folds his hand of tickets, pockets them, and reaches for cigarettes in the inside pocket of his suit jacket. Freddy offers one to Wing. Wing shakes his head, not wanting the distraction of a cigarette for the race. Freddy takes out his matches, a Lychee Gardens Restaurant matchbook, flips the cover to pull out a match, and pinches the match head between the cover and the striker strip. After cupping his other hand protectively around the fire lighting his cigarette, Freddy breathes out, feels a little bit better. He shakes his hand back and forth to extinguish the match and flips the match over his shoulder.

The horse that balked at going into the starting gate has been calmed and controlled into the gate, but Mumma's seen horses balk at the gate so many times she can't count. She can't help but think about her kids, how they sometimes balk at the gate, each child standing in line. What if the gate opens and one of her kids won't leave the gate? What are they thinking about when they balk at the gate? Is something waiting for them after the first furlong? What about the critical final turn before they head for the finish line? What's happening to those kids when they're out running the track before they come home?

Nope, don't think about that now, Mumma tells herself, not here, not when I'm having this damn capital C, Curse day. Smoke swirls around, people so close and so loud, "gotta go into the barn and look them right in the eye or you're throwin' money down the drain," "Jackie, she's already twelve, yeah, she's still dancing, oh she's got a cute little figure," then, "Get your programs, programs, get your programs here," "PepSi, ice cold PepSi," boys in canvas high top sneakers running up and down the cement stairs, holding stacks of racing forms, balancing large metal trays filled with paper cups of soda, and as the horses are finally lined up in the gate, Mumma looks down and notices her smart purse is smoking.

"And, They're off!" The Public Address system crackles as the starting gate opens, horses bolt forward, and the eyes of the crowd pounce the track.

Mumma opens her purse wider, sees a smoking matchstick on top of her Kleenex-wrapped Kotex. Just as she reaches into her purse to remove the match, all the paper products ignite with the match, and candle-size flames erupt from her purse.

"...and, they're coming to the clubhouse turn, and at the clubhouse turn, it's Blue Hawaii leading with the rail, and three-quarters of a length behind..." bodily, the crowd follows the race past the grandstand, and around the first corner of the track. Without thinking, Mumma reaches into her purse and throws the flaming Kotex in an arc onto the ground in front of her. To Mumma's horror, three seconds after ignition, the flames still grow, combine forces, so Mumma stomps on the flames, left right left right, her smart navy pumps pummelling the spongy base of the fire, until there's nothing left but grey ash covering bits of Kleenex and the burnt remains of a greatly reduced Kotex sanitary napkin, streaked grey and black. One of the napkin's fasteners has managed to free itself from underneath in the scuffle, and lies white and intact, like a weak limb attached to the pad.

Mumma grabs a breath that quickly escapes her open mouth.

Not daring to even think about people's faces surrounding her, Mumma reddens, her hairline feels like someone's running a welding bead over her forehead, her face erupts a slick moisture of sweat. Mayday, Mayday her pelvic floor screams.

With her tiny right foot, Fairy toes the sooty pad until it falls off the cement ledge of the stadium floor seating, and lands right underneath the seat in front of Mumma, where Freddy sits, the pad now completely hidden. The race thunders across the backstretch, wholly capturing Freddy's attention and Wing's. And everyone's around them, all of them completely wrapped up in the sights and sounds of the race, the horses' kinetic energy taking each viewer's senses hostage.

Fairy's arm nudges gently against Mumma's arm, and her hand pats the back of Mumma's hand. Fairy reaches into the left hip patch pocket of her shirt jacket, discreetly slides a white Kleenex-wrapped package into Mumma's empty purse. Fairy smiles at Mumma and says, in Chinese, "Oh wow."

Number 117. Almond Guy Ding

Jane steeps in her claw-footed bathtub, one leg stretched out along the bottom, the other slightly bent. Her face towel drapes over the edge like the paper label of a tea bag resting over the lip of a white teacup. She holds her palms up and studies her fingertips. Raisin-like ridges on water-bloated pink. Peanut fingers, she thinks, that's what I used to call them. Peanut fingers and almond eyes.

At about the time Jane discovered her peanut fingers, her Auntie Li-Ting said, "Janie, you have almond-shaped eyes." Not really knowing what an ah-mund looked like, Jane never did get it right. "I have peanut eyes," she told everyone at her cousin Paul's wedding. But she didn't like the way they laughed when she said that, didn't like the way everyone kept asking her again and again, what kind of eyes do you have, and laughed when she gave the same answer, the flower girl with the nut-shaped eyes.

Jane dips the face cloth into the still hot bath and brings the towel to her face, rivulets run warm down her arms. How am I going to make it through the weekend? Jane blinks, lets the nubby warmth of the towel soothe the corners of her eyes. As soon as she got off the phone with Auntie Li-Ting, she called Mumma.

"But Jane, if she had anywhere else to go, she wouldn't ask. It's only one weekend."

"So, why can't I put her on the greyhound to visit you?"

"You offer her that?"

"No."

"Too late. It's only one weekend. Just don't go grocery shopping with Li-Ting. She's a little light-fingered around the bulk hard candies, oh, and the plastic bags in the produce department."

"Oh God."

"And don't take her to a restaurant where they put sugar packets on every table."

"This is a nightmare."

"Don't be so sensitive. You're the only family she has in Calgary. I don't blame you but one weekend. Janie, this is costing you money. You shouldn't call long distance for this."

Auntie Li-Ting yelling at Jane when teaching her how to make lemon meringue pie for her Brownie badge.

"Mumma?"

"What?"

"Is she really related to us?"

"Of course she is. We just like to pretend she isn't."

Dissatisfied with her talk with Mumma, Jane dialed the phone again.

"Hi, Auntie Moe."

"Is that my favourite thirty-one-year-old niece?"

"It's your only thirty-one-year-old niece."

"Yes, but still my favourite. Janie! How are you?"

"Auntie Li-Ting is coming to stay with me this weekend."

"Really? Oh wow. Time to get out the ice skates and bikini, Hell's frozen over," Auntie Moe laughed, "Busy times, don't go grocery shopping," she added, her singsong voice a gentle warning.

Jane didn't think Auntie Moe would have a perfect solution, but she kept her aunt on the phone for over forty minutes, looping and looping back in the search for one.

"Seriously, Auntie Moe. Any ideas, really. Any at all, let's try spitballing this. You've always got great ideas, Auntie Moe, let's get creative. Please, let's find a way for your favourite thirty-one-year-old niece to keep her sanity and for Auntie Li-Ting to be happy too. Where's our happy ending, what does it look like? That's the goal. How do we draw the line from A to B, from right here right now, to there?"

"Oh Janie," Auntie Moe said slowly and evenly, "Auntie Li-Ting is coming to stay with you, and soon, but only for a short while."

"I wish it was you living in Calgary, coming to stay with me this weekend," Jane said.

"You wish it was me who had bugs and a fumigator coming?" Auntie Moe laughed. "I'd love it if I was staying with you this weekend, wouldn't that be fun? But Brian and I are going hiking at South Mountain Park on Saturday morning."

"Say hello to Uncle Brian for me."

"He still talks about all those years ago when you fell asleep at the Drive-in, both hands holding onto that Berlitz book. Good times. Jane, I think you're his favourite thirty-one-year-old niece too."

"Also his only one."

"Still," Auntie Moe said encouragingly, "still his favourite. Buck up, Sweetie, it's only one weekend."

As soon as she got off the phone with Auntie Moe, Jane retreated to the bath. Turning the silvery steel fixtures, Jane tests the temperature with her finger and holds her face cloth in the hot water. She lays the towel just under the lip on the far edge of the tub, and moulds her shoulder blades slowly against the warm terry.

Drip. Drip. Who would tell a five-year-old that her great-grandmother was gored to death by a water buffalo?

Drip. Drip. "Water and oil," Dad said, as kindergarten Jane lay between her parents, after dreams, those bad thinks, of an old woman, the Chinese-iest-looking old woman, being stabbed by the horns of the buffalo at Al Oeming's Alberta Game Farm.

Drip. Drip. "Li-Ting is just too damn vivid for this sensitive soul," Dad said, pulling the edge of the covers over Jane's body, "She's your sister... Well?"

"   "

"Well?"

"Half-sister," Mumma said, switching off the lamp.

"No problem," Leo said, "We didn't have anything planned for the weekend anyway. In fact, I'll just put all this junk in the basement and get the guest room ready for her."

Jane holds on to both edges of the tub, trying to turn the tap shut with her big toe. Damn that Mrs. Lin and her bug-infested dried Chinese mushrooms, she thinks. Damn her for going to visit her sister in Vancouver and turning up the heat for her jade plants. Damn those dumb bugs, multiplying and crawling along the pipes at the Elders' Mansion.

"Everyone's apartment. They have to foomigate," Li-Ting said excitedly, "Bug spray all over, to kill it. They say Mrs. Lin's place is worse. Especially the kitchen cupboards. Little brown bugs everywhere."

"Have you seen any in your apartment?" Jane asked.

"No. But my eyes not too good. They have to spray everywhere. It's no good for my breathing. If there is anyone else, I would not ask."

"No, no. Of course you can come stay with us."

"I wouldn't ask, but my breathing."

Breathing is Auntie Li-Ting's obsession. She gravitates to cheesy cotton dresses so her skin can breathe. Rolls her cotton tube socks down into big white ankle doughnuts so her leg muscles can breathe. She even cut the toes out of all her shoes and slippers. A while ago, she had offered to do Jane's shoes, but Jane declined, as Li-Ting's white foot puppets flexed upward, inhaling deeply.

"OK. What bus goes to your house?" Li-Ting asked.

"I don't know. Why?"

"I need to know what bus to take. I will have to transfer, I think. Maybe even go on the train," she said, hesitating.

"No, I'll come get you. Leo and I will come and get you."

"I don't wanna be a bother."

"It's no trouble."

"You sure?"

"Yes."

"OK. I see you tonight then. After dinner. I have leftover to finish."

"Auntie?"

"What?"

"How long are they, uh, spraying?"

"Oh. They spray tomorrow. I go home Monday. Sunday night if you like."

"No. Monday's fine. Or however long."

Jane licks tiny beads of moisture forming on her upper lip. Fumigating for bugs. Five years of renting shared halls and walls, Jane shudders. This was supposed to be the do-nothing weekend, the first in months. Maybe the baking cookies in the nude weekend. Maybe the checking into the Westin Saturday night weekend. Maybe the sex on the breakfast nook weekend. Under the breakfast nook?

Enough, Jane thinks, grabbing the chain between her toes and pulling. It's a lost weekend. Why didn't I think fast enough to suggest treating her to the greyhound for a visit with Mumma and Dad? Why am I acting like a monster child? Why am I so hopelessly suburban — the breakfast nook?

"Pulease," Jane says to the walls. Standing up, she listens to the vortex, the part soap-part Jane scum whirls out of the bottom of the tub.

Lying on top of the quilt, Jane soaks in the pinky skin, bone-less body feeling from being too long in the tub. She wraps herself in Leo's blue terry bathrobe that gathers around her feet, feet slippered in his sheepskin moccasins. The robe smells of him, his apple soap, his bergamot, cardamom and autumn leaves cologne. Jane holds the lapels up to her nose, savouring the forest floor assurance of his smell.

"It's seven o'clock. We better get rolling, Jane."

"Just a few minutes."

"C'mon, it'll be fine. Don't worry. And hang up my robe when you're finished with it?"

"I always do."

The neon signs roll by as Leo drives north on Macleod Trail. Jane reads the names silently, The Co-Operators, Un Poco Picante, The Flamingo, 7 Seas. Suddenly, she bats at Leo's arm, and points out the window.

"Hey, did you see that?"

"What?" Leo gives her a full profile of the Barclay face. The Barclays of Bragg Creek, of hostelling in Canada, as set into the land as the Rockies, the 100-year lease in the national park, the cottage at the lake. Jane catches his hazel-grey eye and the line drawn from his nose, over his lips and across the jaw line. "He's so good-looking," she told her friend Sandi when she first met Leo, "it makes my teeth hurt."

"The China Garden Restaurant, featuring the Lucky Dragon Room," she says, jabbing at the passenger door window with her thumb.

"So?"

"Remember, in Spokane? 'The Ling-nan Restaurant and the Purple Lantern Room', 'The Jade Palace and the newly renovated Lotus Blossom Room', 'The Bamboo Garden Restaurant featuring the Sin-Loc Room'. Remember? And I said to you, 'Well, what do they think people are going to imagine goes on in those rooms?' I said, 'when probably those are just the names for the lounges'."

"Oh yeah," half of Leo's face smiles at her, "I remember, but you didn't want to stop and find out for sure."

"Well. You know I hate that kind of stuff. Panders to a stereotype. For God's sake, the Sin-Loc room?"

"Hmm. I think you're being a bit sensitive. What difference does that make, just someone marketing their business, right?" Leo turns to face Jane, but finds the back of her head, her hair flickering inky blue under the passing neon lights.

Sensitive, people always say I'm sensitive, Jane muses. Mumma called Jane "little Miss Foon Kee Bean Cake" when bathing her, Jane bowing back and forth under the weight of her mother's hand, the soapy towel rubbing her back pink. "You're so sensitive, Jane," Mumma, Dad, her siblings, her husband, everyone tells her, as if they are more comfortable, more adept at being Jane than she is. [Note: Jane doesn't appreciate that it takes some sensitivity to tell someone they're being sensitive, more sensitivity, say, than telling someone they're being a pita (pain in the ass).]

As they reach the crest of cemetery hill on Macleod Trail, Jane spies the shadowy profile of the pagoda in the Chinese graveyard. Her great-aunt and great-uncle are buried here, and the only memory Jane has of visiting their grave is a black-and-white photo of herself, six years old, holding flowers beside the gravestone. She has never told Leo. She's seen his family photo albums. Everything is outdoors. Hiking, canoeing, diving off a floating dock. A photo of everyone standing around a firepit in winter, holding wooden snowshoes. Rows of white teeth and Kool-Aid smiles. Everyone wears red plaid, even the dog.

Turning on to Fourth Avenue, Jane's shoulders clench. The streets in Chinatown are so narrow. Leo moves around a delivery van, double-parked, and brakes suddenly. A man runs out in front of the car with his hand held up to command the car to stop. It's always like this, Jane thinks, one-way, one-way, flashing four-way flashers, people running out onto the streets. On the occasional family visits to Calgary's Chinatown when Jane was small, she perched at the car window holding her glasses in her hand to see the blurring swirl of lights from the traffic and the shop signs. Now, she looks straight ahead, hands clasped one on top of the other, arms pressed close to her body.

"Would you relax?" Leo wraps his right hand around her two as he steers toward the Elders' Mansion. "Look. There she is. I wonder how long she's been standing there."

Li-Ting carries two brown paper shopping bags, with twine loop handles. Under the wispy frizz of her salt-and-pepper perm, her eyes keenly peel the street. Five feet tall, and shrinking, the grey chenille cloche with a crocheted flower adorning the left side appears to be keeping Li-Ting's sparse hair from scattering in all directions. Sandwiched between the glass of the apartment's entrance way, Li-Ting looks preserved. Her burgundy ski jacket is unzipped, revealing a white Minnie Mouse Disneyworld tee shirt, under a short grey cardigan. The tee shirt, a souvenir from Jane's parents, signals the importance of the visit. The hem of the shirt peeks out under her jacket, skirts black polyester pants. On her feet, Auntie Li-Ting wears thirty-year-old semi-opaque olive plastic overboots with an elastic frog closing. From the car, Jane sees the white ovals of her aunt's socks peeking out from under the toe caps.

While Jane pivots her legs out of the car, Leo's already bounding up the stairs, two at a time. Li-Ting props the glass door open with her buttocks, swinging the bags outside in front of her. Jane waves and Auntie Li-Ting holds up her two bags.

Leo approaches, and Li-Ting's head recoils. He bends slightly and wraps his arms around Li-Ting, who stiffens as if lassoed. Li-Ting turns her head up at Leo, stunned, still holding her bags. Leo bends down and says something as he loops his hands into the bags' handles with her hands. They struggle. The curve of Leo's smile falters, as they both hang on, tugging gently on the bags. Finally, he relents, and shrugs his shoulders at Jane, his face and palms-up hands ask, What'd-I-do? Li-Ting takes off down the stairs in front of him, a firm grasp on her bags, her eyebrows knotted. Jane feels a sour stroke curl through her stomach.

"Hi Auntie, I'm sorry we're late."

"Not so late. Only forty minutes. Is not so cold outside."

"Li-Ting, we would have rung up for you," Leo offers, opening the back door.

"Auntie, come sit in the front," Jane says, quickly positioning herself by the back door.

"No. I sit in the back with my bags."

Jane closes the back door, conscious of the ache in her cheeks from smiling. Leo rounds the driver's side of the car. He rubs his fingers under his nose and grimaces.

"Euuwww," he mouths over the car roof, then whispers, "I think there's food and stuff in one of those bags."

Jane smiles at him and lets an airy "shhh" escape between her teeth.

In winter, Auntie Li-Ting wraps medicated bandages around her torso and knees to ease the stiffness. She keeps the bandages in an old tin coffee canister, until the Fall, when she doctors them with a homemade brew, mixed and stored in a Johnny Walker Red Label bottle. There are seven sets of bandages, much like days of the week panties, and once a week, every week until the May long weekend, Li-Ting washes and re-medicates the bandages, sluices them, straight out of the bottle. Li-Ting's formula is a secret, but to Jane, it smells of Tiger Balm ointment, menthol, aromatic barks soaked in whisky, nutmeg, and a good measure of Absorbine Jr. Finally, to complete the recipe, an undertone of a generous shot of something that smells like Worcestershire sauce. The medication, even upwind, insists on attention, and diffused by the car's heater, the smell becomes pore deep.

Jane swears Auntie Li-Ting asks her the same questions every single time they talk. She never knows any of her local Chinese-Canadian contemporaries that Auntie Li-Ting knows.

"How about Carol Low, you know her?"

"No," Jane says, "I don't think I know her either."

"Well, she has two girls. So cute, Janie. They come to have tea with Mrs. Soo every Friday. Then Carol, she get her mother's grocery list and goes picks up everything she wants. Ai-ya, so nice, that girl."

"Mmmmm." Stopped at a light, Jane sends Leo her I-can't-stand-this look.

"And Jennie Ng, on my floor. Her nephew is doctor at the Foothills Hospital. He wants her to come live... big house....
"Do you?"

"What? Pardon me?"

"Do you know his wife?"

"No, I don't think so."

"Well, she.... and their children... so nice.... how long?"

"Four years," Jane says, "we've been married four years."

Leo reaches across to hold Jane's hand. Jane clenches her teeth, anticipating.

"You better have babies soon, Janie. You are so late marrying. You not eighteen any more you know."

Leo's hand lets go of Jane as he covers his mouth, coughing.

As they pull into the garage, Jane pushes the car door open and tries hard not to gasp. Leo leaves his window open a crack, stands beside the car, "Phew." Jane opens the door for Li-Ting. Her olive boots flap-flap against the cement pad.

"Auntie, your bags."

"Yes. You bring them, Janie."

Jane stands with Leo at the kitchen sink, massaging her cheeks with both hands as Auntie Li-Ting settles into the guest room. Leo wraps his arms around Jane, kisses the top of her head and rests his chin there. They hear footsteps on the kitchen hardwood and wheel around together. Auntie Li-Ting rubs her palms together, as though she knows something they don't. On her feet she wears red satin slippers, the toes carefully cut out, with dragons beaded on the tops in gold, blue, white, orange and pink bugle beads. The dragons perch on white cotton sock half-moons, and when she flexes her toes, Auntie Li-Ting's dragons dance. Jane stiffens as Leo continues to hold her closely. She feels her face turn red. "How about something to drink?" she suggests.

"Oh good idea," Leo says, letting go. "Li-Ting? How about you?"

"Oh, I like a cup of tea," Li-Ting says.

Leo returns from the dining room, dropping a skinny heel of a bottle on the kitchen table, and retreats to the cold room in the basement for mix. As Jane fills the kettle, Li-Ting dampens a dishcloth and starts to wipe the counter tops.

"A grown man like that. You think he would know how to take a bath," Li-Ting says.

"Pardon me?"

"He smells bad. Like he leaves the soap on and doesn't wash it off."

"That's cologne, Auntie. Men's perfume. Like Florida Water."

"Oh no, is not. And he has to hang himself all over people. That's Bee-oh. That's Leo." She laughs, "Funny, neh?"

Jane's mouth drops, but can't suppress one giggle. "Auntie, that's terrible. I mean it." She frowns at her aunt who shrugs.

"And you, drinking booze. No wonder..." Li-Ting rolls her lips inside her mouth.

"No wonder what?"

"No, no. But Janie, you have —" She stops abruptly as Leo returns to the kitchen.

"You're sure, Li-Ting?" Leo asks, sloshing vodka over ice and topping two glasses with tonic water. She frowns as she watches him stir the ice around with his index finger. Looks away when he pops his finger in his mouth and slowly pulls it out.

"No. I'm sure," Li-Ting replies.

The kettle whistles and Jane swirls hot water in the bottom of the Brown Betty. She takes a box of assorted teas out of the cupboard, and flips through the box, "I have cinnamon, mint, chamomile, orange spice, and Darjeeling. That sounds kind of Chinese-y, Darjeeling. What would you like?"

Auntie Li-Ting takes one of the flat foil packets from the box and says, "What this?"

"It's tea. Tea bag tea."

"You don't have gun jam or pu-erh neh cha?"

"No, I guess I pitched it," Jane says, remembering the black broken sticks in the mayonnaise jars Mumma brought down from Edmonton and Jane threw out soon as Mumma went home.

"Tea should be loose, stored in a glass jar."

"Well, we don't have a tea ball."

"A Chinese girl without a tea ball? A Chinese girl without a tea ball? A Chinese girl —" "without a tea ball," Leo interrupts, "is like a day without sunshine." He laughs, fist bumps the air, pleased with himself.

Li-Ting puckers her lips to one side. "If I knew, I would have brought some tea for you from Chinatown," she says quietly, "That's where you should buy your tea."

"But Auntie, it's so far away from here."

"I know."

After Li-Ting retires, Leo turns out all the lights in the living room while Jane rinses the dishes. A brackish scum floats on top of the contents of the white teacup. Jane pours out the amber liquid. A thickish green-amber ring remains near the lip of the cup. Turning on the tap, Jane rinses the tea residue out of the bottom of the cup, then pours her watery drink down the drain.

Hours later, there's a knock on Jane and Leo's bedroom door.

"Hallo," with each knock, "Hallo. Hallo."

Leo wakes up first. "What's wrong? Hello. Li-Ting, are you all right?"

"Oh. Yes. I need to know where to catch the bus to Chinatown."

"What? What time is it?"

"Seven oh clock. How long it will take me to get there?"

Leo clears his throat. "No. That's OK. I'll take you," he whispers in his morning voice.

Jane keeps her eyes closed, her breath steady.

"No, no. I don't want to be any trouble. Is Jane up?"

"No, she isn't."

"Wake her up. She knows what bus to take."

Jane rolls on to her back. "Auntie, we'll take you. It's no trouble."

"Oh. You are up, Janie. I don't want to be any trouble."

"Just give us a while to get ready. Where? Why do? Auntie, are you worried about your apartment?"

"I have seniors tai chi classes in the church basement this morning. I don't want to be late."

"Oh. OK. We'll be ready in a bit."

"My classes start at nine-thirty."

"OK. We'll get you there in time. We'll be ready in a bit." Jane listens to the dragons dance away from the door.

"I don't get it," Leo whispers, "If she's up this early, she would have beat the fumigators off the mark."

Jane puts her pillow over her face.

"But I guess she needed to get settled here, with her stuff," Leo continues. "You think she might have said something last night."

Jane pulls the covers over the pillow.

When they descend the stairs, half an hour later, Leo and Jane find Li-Ting standing in the front hall, hat on, purse looped over her forearm. She fans one side of her ski jacket open and shut.

"Li-Ting, it's Saturday morning, it'll only take twenty minutes to get to Chinatown."

"I don't want to be late," she says.

"Auntie Li-Ting, did you have any breakfast?"

"No. I don't want to be any trouble. I don't think I should eat your food."

"Auntie, please. Take off your coat. We'll have some breakfast, and then we'll go. I promise you won't be late."

Li-Ting smiles, "Well, you are up now. You can come to class with me."

....

"Why don't you just tell them you don't understand Chinese?" Leo says without taking his eyes off the row of diminutive elderly Chinese women in front of them. They take turns talking to Jane in Chinese, smiling, asking her questions and waiting for a reply. Auntie Li-Ting ditched Leo and Jane as soon as they arrived. She talks to another group of men and women in the kitchen of the church basement, chatting excitedly, and pointing in their direction and laughing.

Because I don't know what else to do other than stand here, and pay attention politely, until Mumma bails me out, Jane thinks. That's what I've done my whole life. At least I'm too tall for cheek pinching now. She doesn't answer his question, but smiles and politely turns for a moment to acknowledge Leo as if she doesn't understand him either.

There are about thirty older men and women, but it sounds like sixty. She looks at a white-bearded man with a Detroit Tigers baseball cap, studies the waffle weave triangle of long underwear peeking out from his shirt collar. Two women stand with their hands behind their backs, jade and gold earrings pull long holes in their thin earlobes. Jane surveys the room of old Chinese people, wonders what personality and life wrote on the pages of each of their lives leading up to this day, silently criticizes herself for being so ignorant of her own cultural history. She exhales, feels she comes up short, a runt dividend, a disappointing return in this room of investors in the Sacrifice for Future Generations fund, all the hard work and selfless reinvestment sunk into hope for a Big Payoff.

Auntie Li-Ting joins them, and holding on to Jane's arm, pats it as she speaks Chinese. Whatever she says satisfies the group, which disperses, some laughing behind the bony hands they hold over their mouths.

"You see that man there?" Li-Ting asks in a loud whisper.

"Don't point, Auntie," Jane whispers.

"His daughter-in-law ran off with a man. Left three children with his son. Ran off with a lo-fahn," she says at Leo.

"Shhh. Auntie."

"It's OK," Li-Ting says, pointing at the man with her thumb, "he knows."

An old man in an argyle cardigan mounts the Sunday school stage, and the seniors move to form horizontal rows on the basement gym floor in front of him. Li-Ting takes Leo and Jane, one on each arm, up to the front row.

"I don't like looking through everyone's behind," she tells them.

Years of ballet and jazz dance classes make it easy for Jane to follow the slow, fluid motions of the instructor. A set form of movements, silently executed, without pauses or strain of any kind. Jane feels her body relax, as the class turns away from the stage. She matches her curving motions to the people around her. Leo looms head and shoulders above the group. What he lacks in flowing execution, he more than makes up in enthusiasm, his broad grin contagious in the semi-circle around him. Leo shrugs and turns 180 degrees when he realizes he is the only one in the room facing east.

In the coatroom at the end of the session, Jane sits beside Auntie Li-Ting, refreshed by the tai chi class and the budding hopeful insight that anticipation can be worse than outcome — so far, so, not so bad. Leo joins them with some papers in his hands.

"Hey, that was great," he says, "You know, Jane, they have classes on weekdays at five. I thought we should check into them."

"Now?"

"We don't have to right now," he says, "but let's grab a bite to eat while we're down here."

"Sure," Jane says slowly, "a restaurant in Chinatown. OK. Good."

"And afterward," Li-Ting suggests, "we walk around Chinatown. Do some shopping. Buy a few grocery."

"No," Jane says, loud and fast, "I mean. Uh-oh. No, I think I left the iron plugged in. We should go home and check."

"I'll go home and meet you later," Leo offers.

"No," Jane responds quickly, "No, I, uh, we all should go. And I told Sandi I'd call her around lunchtime." Looking at Auntie Li-Ting, she confides, "My friend, she's got too many good-looking admirers and big business deals on every single burner, and sometimes she just needs someone to help her back up from the stove and take a longer view."

"Less go, then," Auntie Li-Ting says, standing up and rubbing her palms on her pant legs.

"Wait," Leo says, "No use in all of us going home. Li-Ting, would you like to have lunch and shop with me this afternoon?"

"I don't want to be any trouble."

"I've never been shopping in Chinatown," Leo says, "You can show me the Sights." [Note: This is true, Leo's never been shopping in Chinatown. Jane and Leo have attended exactly one local Chinatown festival, with a market and lion dances, martial arts demonstrations and men offering to translate people's English names and write them in Chinese calligraphy. They didn't shop, but Leo happily carried his long strip of paper around all afternoon, and when he walked by a poster on a travel agency's window that had the word, Barclay, in English, the Chinese calligraphy for Barclay on the poster looked nothing like any characters on his name tag. "What do you think this says?" Leo asked Jane. She replied, "Stay away from our women."]

"But Leo."

"No buts, Jane," Leo says firmly. "Take the car and go home. Talk to Sandi. And check the iron," he says, "Li-Ting and I will have a great old time, I'm sure."

About "the great old time," Auntie Li-Ting looks less than fifty percent convinced, but from the "we'll see" jut of her lower lip, Jane knows she will go home alone.

"Fine," she says, "I'll come and pick you up. When and where?"

"No, that will cramp our style," Leo says, taking Li-Ting's coat off the brass hook and holding it for her. "We'll grab a taxi." Li-Ting smiles as she clamps her cloche down over her forehead.

....

Well what's the worst thing that could happen to them, Jane thinks, Leo signs us up for tai chi after work? She perches on her kitchen nook bar stool, flips through the pages of *Bon Appétit*. Jane subscribes to a number of glossy food magazines, more of a reader of cookbooks than a cook who enjoys reading. Leo will keep Auntie in check. She flips the pages faster, closes the back cover and throws the magazine on the kitchen counter. Jane pulls from the stack of new magazines in front of her and wills away the images of Leo bringing home a Trojan horse box of dried Chinese mushrooms, legions of Asian brown bugs overtaking their cozy home; of Leo mesmerized by barbeque ducks lacquered by smoke and heat to a deep mahogany colour, Leo glued to a spot in front of the heated glass display case where the ducks hang by butcher string, while Auntie Li-Ting and all the other shoppers in the big queue at the Chinese BBQ House wish the big tall lo-fahn would just get out of the way; of Leo and Auntie Li-Ting enthusiastically rummaging through a plastic bin of bloody contraband turtle fins, then two policemen loading the greengrocer, Auntie Li-Ting, and Leo, all handcuffed with white plastic zip ties, hands (still turtle bloody) wrapped in plastic evidence bags, into the cage at the back of the police van, the TV camera footage also showing the other evidence bags held up by the nitrile-gloved policeman, to contain a handful of White Rabbit candies and a small roll of plastic produce bags.

Zingg-bang. The screen door hits the doorframe, followed by wiry vibrations. Jane inhales deeply, breath escapes through the O of her mouth.

"Hi! Boy did we have a good time," Leo calls from the front hall. "We saw. Everything." Two red-cheeked smiles enter the kitchen. Leo and Auntie Li-Ting wear the same thick white tube socks. They each carry several plastic bags, some pink and some white, all bulging and exaggerating the red Chinese calligraphy printed on their sides.

"Jane," Leo continues, "there were these dried fish that looked like they'd been cranked through an old-fashioned wringer washer. Must have been smoked or cured, because they were just lying there, no wrappings, in open cardboard boxes, big flat things, flat, flat, flat. But the best, and I mean the best thing had to be these boxes filled with dried plants. And the lids were all plastic so you could see inside. And on top, God, I still can't believe this, a little shrivelled up dried lizard. A real honest to God dried lizard in every box."

Something the cereal companies should think about test marketing, Jane muses. She shakes her head. Leo, my love, you can be such a turd — big hairy deal, dried up lizards. Leo, she says to him in her head, You should know that in the wonders of Chinatown context, dried lizards are chicken pickin's. You should be there when they're shaving dead pigs for roasting, she thinks, real honest to God dead pig shaving.

"Really?" she says, "Did you buy one?"

"No. They cost twelve bucks. And Auntie Li-Ting says it's the wrong season. No good," he mimics, moving his head as if he is being rotated from the nose in half-turns.

Auntie Li-Ting smiles. "Your Leo. Good shopper. Knows his price. Asks good question. Not bad for lo-fahn."

"Auntie —"

"No. No insult. I go wash my hands."

"Jane, come look," Leo whispers. He lifts a large package wrapped in brown paper out of a bag and places it on the kitchen counter. He's got Christmas morning eyes.

"Oh, geez. Leo. Gross." Jane feels the skin on her arms bump up coldly. Without feathers, it looks especially grotesque, from its brilliant red comb to its claw-tipped feet, the legs covered in peeling patches of yellow bumpy skin.

"Isn't it great? And it's not even eviscerated. So we'll do that."

Jane skims her mental dictionary, eviscerated...viscerated... viscera! "Euwww," she recoils. "No, no. Thank you. No. You are on your own. Cheque please, I am outta here."

"But Li-Ting says there might even be eggs inside," he whines.

"Look. It's not that I haven't seen dead chickens before. I've been to the farmer's market, went every Saturday when I was little. And Chinatown. It's just Mumma never brought them home. I mean, look at it. It looks like a, well, like a dead animal."

"This is a compromise. Li-Ting wanted to bring home a live chicken. Can't you see me, bundling a live chicken into a cab? I mean the comic possibilities, fantastic, but no, I knew that was going too far. See, you can trust me. But she really wanted one. She says they don't let her have them in her apartment. She even said I could hold its feet while she sli—"

"Stop! Stop. I get the picture. Thank You for not bringing home a live chicken, I guess. But I don't wanna touch this thing." Jane makes chopping motions with her hands, "And will you cut off, you know, the top and bottoms, so it doesn't look so —"

"Much like a dead bird."

"Yeah."

With Leo's prodding, the bluish membrane covering the eye peels open, revealing a wet shiny marble of an eye. As he pokes around more, the red comb wiggles.

"Sorry. No can do. Li-Ting says she cooks it whole just like this. Well, without the guts. She wants to make a feast for us. C'mon, get into it." Leo gingerly grasps the bird's beak with his two hands and manipulates the beak open and shut. In a squeaky pitched voice, he says, "See Jane, we don't have lips."

"Knock it off." Jane reaches into the utility drawer and places the stainless meat cleaver on the counter. She takes a plastic cutting board out. Pinching a corner of the chicken's brown paper blanket, she pulls carefully until the chicken slides on top of the board.

"When I come back," she says, "I want this thing looking like something I bought at the Co-op."

"But your aunt wants to cook it for us tomorrow. Whole. Geez, I don't know why you're being so sensitive. Can't you be a good hostess, or niece?"

"Don't tell me how to behave. I'm not eating this chicken with its head on. That's gross. And probably unsanitary."

"Well, talk to your aunt. And what about that song and dance about leaving the stupid iron on."

"   "

"Don't you think she knew?"

"Just chop that stuff off."

"You don't like it. You chop it off."

Yeah. I'll chop it off, Jane thinks, Chop you off. Calm down, she says to herself. Calm down. "I-asked-you-to-chop-it-off," she repeats.

Neither of them hear the red satin dragons slide across the kitchen floor. By the time they smell the bandages, Thwok. Thwok.

Leo and Jane start at the sound of the metal cleaver chopping through bone, vibrating against the plastic board. The chicken lies in three separated sections on the brown paper, feet, body, head, like a drawing where the connections between sections are illustrated by parallel dotted lines. Auntie Li-Ting turns on the tap, and running the cleaver back and forth under the stream of water, says, "It makes no difference. No more head. No feet. I don't want to be any trouble."

"I'm sorry, Auntie Li-Ting. It's just. Well, I am kind of squeamish, you know, sensitive, about some things."

"Many things, Janie. You always been," Li-Ting says. She vigorously wipes the counter.

"So Li-Ting, do we unpack the groceries, or do the chicken first?" Leo asks, rubbing his palms together.

"Chicken first."

Jane fills the bathroom sink with hot water and plunges her hands in, trying to take the edge off the goose bumps. In the mirror, puffiness around her eyes. Puffiness that makes my eyes look like narrow slivers, she thinks, almond slivers, makes me look mean. Jane adds more hot water.

Returning to the kitchen, Jane finds everything gone. The chicken. The bags of groceries. The shoppers.

"Leo? Auntie?"

"Your aunt's getting ready to go out," Leo calls from the living room. "She came out to the front hall and turned on the outside lights." Jane joins him on the sofa.

"What?" she asks, "What's happening?"

"She plays mah jong every Saturday night with three of her neighbours. They're all going to Mrs. Something's son's house for dinner and M.J., as she calls it. He's going to come and pick her up."

"But —"

"Yes, of course, I did offer to take her, but she said he's going to pick up all three of his mother's friends. It was all planned before she came here. Don't worry about it."

"Leo?"

"What?"

"Forty years from now, I'm going to have this selfish, bad-tempered, puffy-eyed, nasty, controlling, dismissive niece who makes me feel like an unwanted guest in her home, right? I mean, she isn't even born yet, but she's waiting for me, big laundry-list of meanness, that whole scenario's just waiting for me, right?"

"Oh probably."

She slaps his arm. He wraps his arms around her, smiling, "I don't know what it is with you and your aunt. You're probably more alike than you think."

Jane disengages her mind from the hugging, thinks, When I am in Leo's thoughts, does he see almond eyes?

....

Jane sits in a tepid bath, trying to acclimatize to the dark, pungent air. A shower is out of the question. The entire length of the oval-shaped shower rod is festooned with brown-stained beige tensor bandages of varying lengths. The effect, to Jane, is like taking a bath at a mummy laundromat.

"I'll never bug you about hanging your pantyhose again," Leo says, coming into the bathroom. "Whoa, baby. These things really stink."

Jane pins her lips together. Li-Ting thinks you stink.

"I know. And they've been washed," she says.

"No."

"Yes. They're for her joints. She puts this stuff on them, let's them dry, then wraps them around her back and knees."

"Oh, the car, right. And the cab ride, huh. No wonder. I thought she wore everything big and loose, because she wants her skin to breathe."

"You just can't measure people with such fine instruments. Everyone's a mass of contradictions."

"Room for two in there?" Leo pulls his tee shirt over his head.

Jane pulls the plug. "I'm getting out. Stinks in here."

....

Jane spends Sunday afternoon at her office. As promised, Auntie Li-Ting will cook Sunday dinner to thank them, but she has banished them from the house, she wants to surprise them. Leo is at a friend's place, helping Bruce with the wiring on his boat.

Jane rests her cheeks in her hands, discouraged by all the In in her In basket. It's not that we don't like each other, Jane thinks, but the smell of those bandages, the cut-out shoes, the chicken, that bluntness, so judgmental and loud. But she means well most of the time. In her own way. And Auntie Li-Ting is a great cook. Maybe she'll make lemon chicken, all moist with that salty crisp skin, lemon juice sprinkled all over. So juicy. Or she's boning the chicken and stuffing it with sweet rice, scallions and Chinese sausage. Or soy chicken, braised whole with soy sauce, and ginger. Maybe chicken simmered with Chinese dates, mushrooms and lily buds. Or hot and sour soup with big, tender pieces of chicken and tiny matchstick-sized vegetables. Mmmm. If I hurry, Jane thinks, I can have a cooking lesson too. Maybe we can find common ground in cooking.

The idea of a Chinese cooking lesson buoys Jane. The extent of Jane's Chinese repertoire is stir-fry, filled with red peppers and broccoli. But Jane's stir-fry's bland, tasting nothing like the food she grew up loving. She rings the front doorbell so Auntie Li-Ting won't be startled, and turns the lock.

"It's just me, Auntie."

Jane waits for the wall of garlic and ginger-infused steam to hit her. It doesn't. She strains to hear the cooking, but no noise comes from the kitchen at all, no tschwshhh of vegetables searing in hot oil, no chop-chop-chop of ginger being minced.

Auntie Li-Ting comes out of the kitchen, wiping her hands on Jane's Kiss the Cook apron.

"Oh. It's you," she says, "You have such a nice kitchen. And you see. I surprise you. Come."

Jane follows her aunt into the kitchen. On the counter, one of Jane's magazines stands open on the counter, propped in a clear acrylic recipe holder. The cooking smell, a clean patrician thyme and peppercorn smell, wafts discreetly from the oven.

"See," Auntie Li-Ting says, pointing at the recipe holder, "I cook this."

This is Cuisine Courante Revisited. Chicken oven-poached in white wine broth. Parsleyed red potatoes, boiled, with a strip of skin peeled from the diameter. Carrots, cut into matchstick-sized pieces, tied into bundles with a strip of blanched scallion and steamed.

"Wow. You did all this."

"But no dessert. We have tea." Auntie Li-Ting opens a wheel-shaped paper package with Chinese writing printed on the outside. Inside, a large compressed cake of fragrant tea leaves. Li-Ting's fingers break off a chunk, and holding it over the mouth of an empty glass jar, the leaves crumble between her deft fingers, quickly filling the jar. "Don't worry. I wash the jar today. With soap. Now, you look at your table. Better than the magazine."

Li-Ting follows Jane into the dining room. "You have many different knife and fork. I just follow the picture."

The table shimmers, formally set. Bread plates. Teacups and saucers. Water glasses. Wine glasses. Rows of gleaming cutlery. Beside one dinner plate is a silver ball with tiny holes puncturing its surface. Li-Ting picks it up and holding Jane's hand, she places the ball in her palm, wrapping her fingers around it. "For you. To make real tea."

Number 19. Egg Drop Soup

[Note: a savoury chicken broth in which some Chinese greens, spinach, or green peas are simmered. Just before serving, it's the chef's skill and technique in dropping one cracked fresh egg into the soup that makes this dish remarkable. That one egg will disperse into a thousand surprising pieces, complementing and bringing out new flavour in all the other ingredients. And if the chef is especially skilled, while people will remember the soup, they'll never forget the singular egg that made everything else happen.]

To see something close to the floor but not on it, Dasha discovers that she must bend her head down, but turn her eyes up in their sockets. She admires the decorative scrollwork at the bottom of the third pew across the aisle from the one she occupies.

"Mother, we should get your eyes checked. You probably need glasses, at least reading glasses," Nancy whispers beside her.

When Nancy travels through Dasha's ears, the words sound fast and choppy, moving chup-chup, up then down, pick after pick, like jagged teeth, a saw-tooth blade. Dasha thinks Nancy spends too much time in the kitchen, so much so that she's come to sound like the beloved Pulse on her chrome electric blender. Nancy's pulse purees words.

Dasha knows she needs glasses. But her eyes work good enough to enjoy seeing pulse-lipped Nancy whenever her mother goes out in public wearing the black-and-silver wire horn rims belonging to Nancy's dead father. They make do, a pretty good fit, and the bit in the top half works best for seeing things close to the floor.

Head down and eyes up, Dasha's eyebrows telegraph the direction of her focus. Across the narrow aisle, one row ahead, Dasha watches a woman's shoes firmly planted, the curtain of skirt rising just above her ankles. Dasha's right forefinger presses against her cheek, her fingertip holds the eyeglasses in place. Thumb cradling the underside of her chin, the rest of her fingers curl near her mouth. Dasha's left arm wraps tighter around the waist of her waistless cotton shift. She trivets her right elbow against the back of her left hand.

Chickens have stronger looking ankles, she thinks, chickens before slaughter. How will Dasha be able to grip tight, keep those legs still enough, her hands moving thickly against panic in motion? Then Dasha remembers she hasn't slaughtered a chicken for over thirty years. Time is playing tricks again. She takes off the glasses, perches the oval pads against the flannel nosepiece inside the burgundy leather glasses case. The black legs folded, the click of the metal clasp on the glasses case reassures Dasha that she's put time back in its box.

Dasha holds her hands before her eyes, palms down, fingers tight against each other. Slivers of light show between her fingers where there were none before. He thought he could tell everything he needed to know about a person by looking at their hands and eyes. Dasha turns her hands over, fewer lines, but the same slivers of light. She thinks she can tell everything she needs to know about a person if they are too quick, agree too easily, to show you their hand.

Rotating the back of one hand into the palm of the opposite hand, back and forth, the warmth and the sound of dry skin washing over dry skin makes the muscles in Dasha's shoulders relax. She presses her hands together, each hand moving in a forward circle, her hands never losing contact with each other, commanded by an invisible rotating axle.

She smells burnt leaves, the salty tang of fermented beans and fish. The back door of the Empire Cafe, Vanguard, Saskatchewan. The grease drum. Wooden crates stacked up the wall, the one on the bottom has a splintered slat. Above the door, a grey metal gooseneck pole, a heavy mesh cage surrounds the light.

She doesn't speak English except the words she learned that day and a very few stray words on the journey that led to today. French, yes, Ukrainian, yes. Russian, fluently. And German, of course. The story of how she comes to be at the back door of the Empire Cafe in Vanguard, Saskatchewan, 1921, secured tightly under the scarf that covers her head, as she raps her fist on the wooden frame of the screen door.

Nancy catches her mother's eye, and looks scornfully at Dasha's hands. Mo-ther, she silently mouths. Nancy raises her gloved finger to her lips, and places a Bible in her mother's hands to quiet them.

Dasha studies Nancy's profile, sees the rise of her husband's cheekbone, the rounded "L" of his mandible. He never asked. How could a grown woman, Dasha, sprout up like a sunflower, or be dispatched over telegraph lines, clicks and dashes sliding off the paper and whirling in the air to form people to walk into Vanguard, Saskatchewan, in 1921? Or was she part of a supplies order carted off a freight train, a drum of lard, check, a sack of flour, check, a woman, check. Dasha smiles. It's not that she wanted him to ask. He thought he could tell everything he needed to know about a person by looking at their hands. And eyes.

It's work that Dasha wants in 1921. A place to stay, food to eat. In 1921, Dasha knows that this means work. She goes to every business in Vanguard. By the time she reaches the last door, the Empire Cafe, it is almost supper time, and there is only a light at the back door, but by then, she does know to point to herself and say, "I want work," after a day of a few shop owners attempting to show her how to see through the smeared mirror of "Not You, I." Finally, "I don't want work, you do, so you say, 'I want work, I want work'," Jeb Olson at the Vanguard Hotel said, pointing at himself.

Bliss opens the screen door at the back of the Empire Cafe. Dasha has seen Chinese men before, but never up close. Her speech forgotten, she stands there, tongue hiding below her lower lip. He swallows hard, lines furrow his forehead, he looks behind either side of her head as if he expects one or more people to be hiding behind her. Dasha looks over her shoulders too, the idea planted in her mind. But there's no one behind the café except her. Bliss's eyes vibrate with his mind's desperate attempt to anticipate the crucial next step, to figure out the set-up. She opens her mouth wide, to force the English words out, and Bliss's eyes grow black, anticipating the scream. At this time of the year, Bliss closes the café at five p.m., more customers for breakfast at four a.m. than the few troublemakers past dark.

"I want work," the syllables rasp against the chords of a dry voice box.

"No work. Sorry."

Dasha opens her mouth wide, the fear in Bliss's eyes contagious.

"Come inside, quick," Bliss says, "Come inside the café," he adds, weakly, as if a woman's scream inside the café is better than one in the alley behind the café. What Dasha remembers is his brown eyes deepening black as the pupils spread over the colour, even after Bliss turns ablaze all the lights, and opens the front door widely. After they arrive in the public part of the café, Bliss walks to the back and locks the back door. He comes out wearing a white jacket with a worn neckline. Dasha never got this far inside the other places. She picks up a rag and pantomimes washing and rinsing a bowl and plate, setting them to dry, as Bliss repeats, "No work. Please go. No work." She wipes a part of the lunch counter and the nearest two tables with strong, competent strokes, then picks up the string mop leaning against the cash register, and makes vigorous esses on the linoleum. Bliss opens the till, sweeps his fingers through the empty coin compartments, and shrugs his shoulders at her. Crescent moons spread wetly under the arms of his white jacket. Bliss is the first person Dasha ever sees who shows fear but doesn't stink from fear. The heat from the ceiling lights inside the café rouses the flies languishing in the bowls of the lamps. Their noise distracts Dasha. Her hands drop to her waist, the handle of the string mop smacking the floor. Whether it's hunger, or the relative paucity of words from this last prospect, or his incomprehensible fear, or the fact that it's already dark and Dasha has no plan other than this one, or all combined, Dasha unbuttons her coat, pulls the scarf off her head, and sits down on a stool at the counter.

Before Bliss can move behind the counter, before Bliss can say, Sorry, we closed, before Bliss can stop himself from saying that in a lit café with the front door wide open, Dasha speaks.

She starts, in French, you do not know who I am but I am a good person and I know of no other way to tell you this, in Russian, I have come a long way and I want to work and this is as far as I have come and about as far as I have money to go, in German, I do not know who you are but if you knew me, you would know that I can work, that I am a good person, and I will wash and clean and better than you, better than anyone you hire.

Bliss retrieves the mop from the floor and leans it against the cash register. He moves behind the counter, and reaches for the water jug and a glass under the counter. He places the full glass on the counter in front of Dasha and hands her a menu. Dasha places the menu on the counter with her scarf, turns her head slightly and her right hand rises to conduct the linguistic symphony of her life.

A deceptively complex score, the words compose themselves one after the other in her mouth, the key of French, Ukrainian, Russian, changing with the scene, the tempo. Bursts of *allegro*, but mostly *andante*. Voice, *sotto voce*, for some scenes her eyes telegraph *bravura*. She looks at that hand of hers, then never looks at it again as her head starts to move very slightly as if keeping time, the words travelling along the curve of movement, rising and falling *dolce*.

Her right hand cradles perhaps a songbird, a loaf of bread, a doll with real hair. Her right hand balls into a fist, her voice imitating a confrontation between two people, *appassionato*, perhaps enemy combatants, or two rivals, possibly a quarrel between a beloved daughter and father. Her right hand recoils and trembles in front of a hardened shoulder, perhaps the recounting of a deep wound reopened, as sudden and scarring as the original assault. Her right hand turns over and lies on the counter, fingers spread, perhaps reconciliation, a resolve to move forward, perhaps both. Elbows bent, she opens her palms on either side of her body. Dasha's voice projects a cocoon of sound that envelopes Bliss and the counter between them. In the filament of words, Bliss hears "Daryna," as the woman turns her hands towards her body, gently cradling her chest bone. "Daryna," she repeats and as she enunciates the word, her hands slowly unfold from her heart.

"Daryna. Daryna." Her right hand strokes her collarbone and glides across her scarf lying on the counter. Maybe the word for scarf, Bliss thinks. Maybe whoever gave her the scarf? Dasha takes the scarf off the counter. Tenderly, she holds the transparent layer of fabric between her fingers to the light, the spools of her words whirling threads into the cloth. "Dar-y-na."

As she puts her scarf down, Dasha notices Bliss turn his head away from her. In French, she concludes, you still do not know who I am, but I am strong, I am a good person and I will work hard, very hard.

Bliss has been translating her eyes, her moving mouth, her hands, but not into words. A clever man by any measure, by the time Dasha has finished speaking, Bliss has figured out that he can surmount the law which prohibits him from hiring Dasha, by all appearances a white woman, by making her a partner in the café, getting all the paperwork right. Years later, when asked by his oldest son to explain what happened when they first met, Bliss will say: language didn't matter, I understood her. No, not what she was saying, but at the same time, I understood all at once. Inside the café, your mother's tongue, the threads of her words, how she spoke with her hands, and the person she is, she connected for me for the first time who I was at that very moment to all the life I had already lived, and all the life I still wanted to live. I knew I wanted to join all my lives with all the lives in your mother. I just hoped to God that she felt that I would be worthy of her. I knew that day that I wanted the threads of our lives to write a story for the both of us.

....

Dasha places the Bible back into the small wooden rack attached to the back of the pew in front of theirs. She opens up the glasses case and holding the end pieces in both hands, makes quite a show of adjusting the glasses onto the bridge of her nose. Just below the left leg of the glasses, Dasha watches Nancy's pencil-lined eyebrow jump, her head shake ever so slightly with the snik of the metal clasp on the burgundy glasses case. Dasha picks up a hymnary, as the Minister requests that people turn to page 235. "That's page 267 in the blue hymn book," the new volunteer translator says, in English.

As they rise to sing, Dasha holds her hymnary as low as her arms and torso will allow. As a point of principle, she will not use the same hymn book as her daughter, or her teenage grandson, Benny Pon. When Dasha sings in the Chinese United Church, she always sings in Chinese.

Number 124. Shark's Fin Soup

Chinese walls surround me on the twenty-eighth floor of Martell McMillan, downtown Edmonton law firm. Evening in my office, I sit cross-legged, stare at my computer screen, tap code into the keyboard I balance on the arms of my chair: Trust Indenture. Ironic, oxymoronic, Trust Indenture, the name of the document I draft. Hereinafter, now therefore, I draft within these Chinese walls. Chinese walls press inward, I feel smaller than a child.

When she was a child, my mother followed the end of the Calgary Stampede parade to the fairgrounds. As an adult, she traps my friends in her spiral stories of the past. She speaks of chicken coops and candy her mother made from dried yams and fishing in the river from a raft. Entranced by these exotic revelations, inevitably, some pie-eyed innocent asks, "What part of China do you come from?" Mumma, so excited she almost jiggles the hook too fast, blurts out, "Calgary. Sixth Avenue, kitty corner to the old Firehall." But the kitty corner stuff no one understands because her laugh uses too much breath.

Chinese walls fit snugly against the papered drywall. Carl Thomas, a new lawyer in the office, came from a law firm that represents the company one of my clients wants to acquire. Carl may have confidential information that should not be revealed to me. I picture Carl, dossiers stamped "confidential" rolled tight into white paper perm rods suspended in the mousse and blow-dry of his remarkable big hair. Otherwise unremarkable Carl came to my office late this afternoon, with his remarkable big hair and his message: "Just wanted to say hullo. No hard feelings, Liz. Don't say a word. You're behind the Chinese wall."

Someone wrote a story, told a story to create Chinese walls, a legal fiction, but Carl put his hands up and felt along an imaginary border by my door. An unremarkable mime too, I thought, as he turned the imaginary key to his zipped lips. I picture Carl grasping the edges of a transparent artifice. I explained to my client that I would not talk to Carl. At the same time, to protect his former client, Carl would not discuss his work with me. Like dogs marking trees, our respective offices become off-limits to each other. Our assistants also cannot talk about work. Carl and I act as though we work independently, separated by physical barriers. The strategy is so much intellectual legerdemain, a little bit more the latter than the former. Chinese walls as transparent artifice. But Business. Is. Business as business. Does. And I am stuck with Chinese walls.

Chinese walls? Taught in law school as a when why and how chapter, but nothing about the name. Too embarrassed to ask, I looked into the origin of the naming, discreetly. Nothing. Perhaps something to do with the Great Wall, so vast that astronauts photograph it from outer space. Or is the slant inscrutability?

"So, you've brought out the old Chinese walls, eh?" Sharing one gypsum office wall with the lawyer next door is almost all I can tolerate of Rick Bulcan. He stands in my door frame, his pocketed fists fanning the pleats in his pants. "You're lucky to have held onto your client," he says, hands in constant motion, squeezing the brass out of the doorknob. "Although, I don't know, maybe not so lucky. Deals like this always turn ugly. Blow up. Then, you just bury yourself in paper and hope the stuff flung by the fan doesn't hit you." He laughs, "But it will. Chinese walls. One day, you're building them, and the next day, you're being sued right down to bare bones. Disbarred. Scorched. Good old Chinese walls," he says, slapping my doorframe. "Hey Liz, can you do this?" he says, flips a grill of imaginary burgers with several turns of his wrist, "You should practice. This has to come to you naturally, you know, like you're eager to ask customers: 'Do you want fries with that?' Hah!" I hear the suckling pops his cigar-nursing mouth makes, and look up to see his back retreating in suspendered animation. "I'm outta here," he calls.

I know his smirk. Every colleague smiles when they say, "the old Chinese walls," "bringing out the old Chinese walls." Rick's voice, earlier in the day, dragging his lunch buddy drift net through the hall, entangling his friends to go for lunch: "Yeah, pretty redundant all right — Chinese walls and a Chinese girl. Made in China."

The imaginary edifice transforms to a warning. Does it? Does it say: Chinese girl, shore up these walls. Check your materials. Use twice as many nails. And support beams. But if your walls prove unwieldy, or too strong, prepare for the mocking you'll suffer. Chinese walls will never come down. Or do all imaginary walls come with anxiety wainscoting?

What a name. In the United States, they now call the same device a screen, or a Cone of Silence. We may soon. I see a black-and-white image of Maxwell Smart, television secret agent, on his shoe phone sitting under the campish glass cone with a cardboard sign, "Cone of Silence." I try to concentrate, tap code into the keyboard: special resolution, carrying on business under the firm name and style. Name and style. The naming of the daily special at the Oriental Moon Cafe.

I am eight years old, walking to the Dan Dee Confectionary for a pop, and to wait for Dad. Only six days and twenty-three hours until my next lesson with torturous Mrs. "pree-tend like thee feengers go float-ting over that pee-ano" Vichalsky. As I round the corner, I check out the daily special at the Oriental Moon Cafe. Not again. I walk next door and pull on the metal bar running diagonally across the screen window, "Drink 7-Up," it says, but that's not my drink.

"Hey Gao Buck, you got the sign wrong. Again."

I call him Gao Buck because Ah Bahk means respected uncle, and Gao is the closest thing to his Chinese name that he and Dad think I will remember. He wears a long grey smock with "Dan Dee Confec." embroidered in red cursive on the chest pocket, and has impossibly black hair for his age that falls in a gentle poof over the edge of his right-eye glasses frame. I smell his smell of cold cream and sugar.

"Gao Buck, it's sweet and sour pork, not sweat and sour. Sweet and sour. No one would order sweat and sour pork."

Gao Buck writes the sign for the Daily Special, in English, for Norman Tsai who runs the Oriental Moon next door. Every day, he prints the special in block letters on a piece of paper, and tapes it onto a plywood sandwich board that stands on the sidewalk. Norman Tsai has terrible printing, worse than a Grade 1 kid. But I've watched him write the daily specials in Chinese on pink pieces of paper he puts into the pockets inside the menus, and he writes those neatly and very quickly. I don't know what the specials are, but I know good penmanship.

Last week, I dragged Gao Buck out to the sidewalk to show him that week's mistake. He bent down, shading his eyes from the sun, and read, "Daily Special — Chop Suey." Before I could reply, a young couple got out of a van in front of the restaurant. She craned her head over the strip of stores like it was the last place in the world she wanted to be, especially doubtful of the restaurant window.

"Are you sure this is the place?" she asked out of the side of her mouth.

"Oh yeah," he said, pointing at the sign. "This has got to be it. Look. Daily Special — Chop Suzy."

He let out a hoot, and throwing his arm around the woman, they sailed into the Oriental Moon.

"Seeee?" I said, stretching that one syllable into an aria of righteous indignation. Gao Buck stood with his arms crossed as I stood in front of him, my finger pointing at the sign, the other hand balled into the non-existent curve of my hip.

"Oh well. Poor Suzy," he said and walked back into the Dan Dee Confectionary.

There is a moist sugary aroma in the Dan Dee Confectionary, like The Old Store. Wooden floorboards wince under the linoleum floor tiles as I walk slowly to the pop cooler. There's no one else in the store, so I won't be rushed. I turn to face Gao Buck, who must smile in his sleep. The idea of sweating, sour pork makes my stomach flip flop.

"You're not gonna change the Sweat and Sour sign. Are you," I say.

"That's right. I'm not changing. Uncle Norman decides on the daily special. People come. They like it. Pineapple chicken ball, egg roll, deep-fried shrimp. You have to give them what they want. I don't decide. Uncle Norman decides."

I turn my back on him and roll my eyes up until my eyeballs hurt.

The lid of the enormous soda pop cooler feels heavy, opens like a casket on hinges that sound like question marks. Near the top, narrow rows of steel with rounded edges suspend glass bottles by their ridged necks. The motor chugs loudly to keep cold rivulets of water running down the bottle sides. The cooler hasn't been filled up, so there's some play in the bottles. I lift them, ever so slightly by the top of their necks, move them around the steel maze. Two orange pops to the very top, a cream soda and a root beer to the middle, one ginger ale to the row of Pepsi-Cola Gao Buck arranges so carefully. Add to that row three grape pops that only dorks and babies drink, for the sweat and sour pork thing. There. A clear path for my bottle, the bottle cap with the pretty picture, the one that calls my name. I move the bottle to the launching pad over on the left, its steel sleeve wrapping three-quarters of the way around the neck. I dig in my jeans pocket as I focus on the coin slot, a round hole mounted vertically against a matching piece of solid metal. I put my quarter up to the coin slot, hold it there for a second with my thumb. I barely move my thumb, the magic tone of coin slotting hollow down a metal slit. Klek, klek. I grasp the cold, wet neck of the bottle. Heave, I hear the scrape of glass on metal. The sleeve falls back to earth. Kchunk. Presto. A Tahiti Treat rabbit.

As I line up the neck in the bottle opener, I read, "Gray Beverages. Bttld. in Canada." I pivot on my heels.

"Hey, Gao Buck. Look at this." I show him the bottle. "If this stuff is made in Canada, how come they call it Tahiti Treat? Do they drink this stuff in Tahiti? Do they really think it's a treat?"

"I don't know, Lizzie." He pauses for a moment. "Maybe. Do you think they do?" He leans on the glass counter top and peers down at the small case boxes of chocolate bars on the shelves inside the counter. "Look at that, eh?" He points to one box of chocolate bars. "Do you think Cubans eat that block of chopped nuts and chocolate for lunch? Do you think that's what they call, Lunch, in Cuba? And look, you eat that," he says, pointing to the brightest box, turquoise, with red letters on a white background, "Do you think pink jelly candy covered in chocolate is what little girls like you in Turkey call, Delight? 'Oooo, gimme a piece of Delight, please!' Do you? Is that what you think they say?"

Gao Buck cups his elbows with his hands and leans on the counter towards me, giving me his "I think you should pay attention" face. My lips press against each other, just like they do when Mumma feels the need to lecture me. "It's just a name, Little One. Tahiti Treat. Cuban Lunch. Turkish Delight. Use your head. It's just a name."

Hmmm, I think, then ask, "Gao Buck, are you coming back to church?"

"Oh, I don't know. Why you ask?"

"You should come back. You know, those people haven't shown up in ages. I don't think they're coming anymore."

"Oh?"

"Nope. They stopped coming. Well, not before they keyed Uncle Malmo's car, and not before they said some really bad stuff, but they've stopped showing up now. But then lots of people like you stopped coming. You should come back."

"We'll see, Lizzie."

"You know what made them stop? Benny Pon's grandma. Yeah, Benny's grandma stood up, one Sunday, right in the middle of the service, just after those men called our dad some really Bad Names when he went to the back to talk to them. She stood up and turned around, and said something to them in some language I don't know. Not Chinese. She pointed her cane at them, and she yelled something, I dunno what. Not many words though, and they took off, like, bam. They just took off, and haven't come back. So you should come back."

"We'll see, we'll see."

....

Benny Pon's grandma, I haven't thought of her in the longest time, white hair in a bob, and the bluest eyes, as the office air conditioning shuts down for the night. She spoke Chinese, wrote Chinese, was a regular at church. She was just one of the other kid's grandmas. I thought she was an old Chinese woman with white hair and blue eyes, never thought otherwise, but now I don't know. Now, Chinese walls obscure everything.

With the air conditioning off, the heat of the day bleeds through the walls and floor of my office. I better not forget to throw out my Styrofoam-plated chef salad on the credenza before I leave. I pull my silk scarf off the coat hanger and tie it loosely around my neck, stiff from sitting all day and most of the night. Is Chinese wall just a name? Is the wall made of rundle stone from a quarry near Canmore, Alberta but covered in tapestries embroidered with Chinese dragons, much the same as souvenir snow globes of Mount Robson are Made in China? Use your head, I think, Is it really just a name? What do I know about Chinese walls? What do I know about China?

"That's a funny question," I hear Mumma saying to me twenty-five years ago. I pick raspberries, try not to get too many scratches on my arms. On all fours, she thins the carrot patch. She kneels back on her haunches and rubs the back of her yellow and green gardening glove gently across her forehead. "What do I know about China? Well, aren't you learning about China in school? You should ask your teacher. Or look China up in the encyclopedia. I don't know anything about China that I wouldn't have to first read about in a book. Nothing important, anyway. What you need to know about China, I'm sure you will learn at school. Go ask your father."

"Dad?"

Dad came to Canada as a little boy, after the first World War. What he remembers about China parallels what I know about Canada at age eight. My house, my dog, my friends. He had a boxer dog, he says, but he doesn't remember its name. Maybe it didn't have a name, he says. "We didn't treat animals the same way you treat Pom-Pom." He remembers being told by Uncle Sonny's mother to follow Uncle Sonny home from the market and school because he could be distracted in an instant, so absent-minded, he left a trail of belongings behind him wherever he went. Dad laughs, "I picked up Sonny's things for ages. One week his books would be on the road, the next week, I'd be picking his sandals out of the gutter." This is not a stretch to believe, as I picture Uncle Sonny sitting on his veranda in the summer, listening to American baseball on his transistor radio, a half-eaten sandwich, paper notes scattered like confetti, and a homemade paper dragon marionette needing to be re-strung lying on the chrome-sided Formica table beside him.

"What about your mom?" I ask. Dad came to Canada to join his father, but his mother stayed in China. "What did she look like?"

He pauses. "I don't remember," he says. "I don't remember what she looked like."

"You don't have a photo?"

"No. I suppose if I did I would remember. I remember her voice, and a birthmark she had on her palm, her left hand, but not her face. Why do you want to know about China?"

"What happened to your mother?"

"Well, a little while after I came to Canada, she died. My father told me she died of a broken heart."

"What does that mean, broken heart? Did she have a heart attack?"

"They told me she died of a broken heart, that's what they told me. But let me tell you about being in Canada."

I hate this part. He always wants to talk about how his father and the uncles came to Canada and went to southern Saskatchewan. After Dad arrived, he went to a parochial school, the only school in town, for the better part of a year, finished one school year, then stopped to work in the restaurant they ran in White Rose. He tells me he had two shirts, one to wear and one to wash. He tells me about the men wearing robes and their polished leather oxfords, with square toe caps, the same shoes that would imprint the floors of the town church, and the fields for the picnic box socials. He tells me about their rallies in Regina, outside Moose Jaw, all over southern Saskatchewan to sell memberships, the fires, and a friend of Uncle Sonny's dad, deaf, trapped one night in an abandoned rail car, waiting for the fire to die down. He tells me that after that night, the deaf man feared the stars in the sky at night, but became even more afraid of being alone in daylight, and square-toed leather oxfords. Dad's tongue and breath can't pull the sound, "kl," particularly in succession, through the chords of his voice box. Instead of listening, I focus on what cookie dough tastes like, smashed windows in the restaurant and the Chinese laundry, sugar and butter, people being attacked in the middle of the day with the irons from their own laundry business, soft raisins and chocolate chips. And the men coming into the restaurant, trying to bait Dad's dad and the uncles into a fight so it could be self-defence, toasted coconut and walnuts.

The bony elbow of eight-year-old me, resting on the table, my hand covers my mouth and my nostrils. I can hear myself breathing. Then Dad winds down, like he always does, and talks about coming to Alberta and meeting "your mother the angel" in the basement of the Chinese United Church. How Grandma, when she met him, wanted to fatten him up with pastries and cream. How he has his own store, but he's concerned that pretty soon, people won't shop that way anymore, so he will have to look ahead for something else. How hard, how very hard you must work, like he does, to get ahead.

"So I don't remember much about China, Little One. But, a song that men building bridges, or temples, or big buildings used to sing. It went, 'Hey-ah, Ho-ah, Guey gum nay koang-ah.' Without big machines to do the work, no cement trucks, no excavators, no cranes, they used manpower, in groups, to do the heavy work. The song gave them the rhythm they needed to pull together. Like tug-of-war."

"What does that mean, that hey-ah ho-ah stuff?"

"Well, that first part is just like 'hey you'. The rest means, 'Did the devil make you poor?' you know, Stupid. Unlucky. Did the devil make you so poor that you have to work so hard?"

....

Outside my window, in the building across from this one, the last floor lit by a row of lights, darkens. I turn to the computer screen and tap, In witness whereof, the parties hereto set their hands and seals. I think, when this file is over, it's over, and I won't have to think about Chinese walls. What I remember about China from school is the Boxer Rebellion, just the name, which always calls to mind my dad's boxer dog and Uncle Sonny's sandals. I set the dredgers a little deeper on the floor of my mind. Studying China in Grade Three meant an afternoon party where the students walked around the classroom in white ankle socks, eating Chinese take-out, with fortune cookies for dessert. And making dragons, gluing elbow macaroni scales, gilt with spray-paint, to an outline of a construction paper dragon.

I save my document and stretch my arms. My glasses are smeared and greasy, I notice, as I rub one, then the other gritty eye. Digging my heels into the carpet, I flex my leg muscles to turn my chair around and organize tomorrow's paper mounds.

Smooth stone Chinese walls. I put my glasses back on, but that only defines the edges of the smooth stone walls more clearly. Grey stone that I don't recognize as western Canadian, but some form of granite. No claustrophobic feeling to cut down, the walls do not even approach ceiling height, but they enclose on three sides to the window I had been facing. A little concrete dragon perches on the top of one side.

I move toward the walls, touch quickly with the tip of a finger, then rest my fingers, my whole hand on the face of the wall. Cool to the touch. I push hard. Sturdy walls, the wall doesn't move. I hike up my skirt. The dragon's bulging eyes censure yet also prod me. I reach up and transfer my weight to both hands, resting on the top of the wall. Swinging my left leg, I catch the top of the wall with my heel and pull myself up. I crouch on all fours along the top of the wall. It takes my weight, is wide enough, so I peer over to the other side of the wall. Garbage piled at the base of the wall, looks as if the wind has blown it there, and it's stuck. Empty bottles, broken glass, paper. Chocolate bar wrappers, some old shoes, and sandals. I hold my arms out for balance and slowly stand tall. My arms start to swoop as I walk, then skip along the wall. My shoulders and hips join in, and I turn and bend my knees. I dance a twisty spiral dance. From my perch on the Chinese walls, I think, sometimes you have to give them what they want.

Number 29. Fragrant Meats with Chinese Baby Greens

"Mumma, What's that turrible smell? What Is that turrible smell? Ooooah! Mumma! What's that Turrible Smell?"

Mumma stands in the hallway bisected by the beige sofa travelling mid-air. Mumma's teeth clench behind her smile as seven-year-old Pen stalks around the living room of The New House. Pen's determined to find the rotting corpse of a feral turrible. There's only the wingback chair in the living room so how hard could a turrible be to find? Slippery hardwood under sock feet, so much fun, and the floor doesn't hide a thing. Not behind these curtain panels. Pen hooks her thumbs under the straps of her green stretchy suspenders with the white teddy bear pattern. Her eyes x-ray all surfaces, her head moves along the length of freshly varnished baseboards, cranes up to the curtain valances, precise fluid alertness. Pen's lips disappear into her frown, inhaling, her chocolate chip-shaped nostrils flare and relax. Flare and relax.

"Where do you want the couch, lady?" asks the man entering the living room at the helm of the beige sofa. Pen detects the man's profile, frowning, then turns her head to enhance the view of the bottom of the sofa.

The quiet man with his hands under the frame at the other end of the sofa, Ken, or at least the guy in the royal blue coveralls with an oval-shaped patch over the heart, an oval-shaped heart patch into which a machine has embroidered "Ken" in loopy white letters, Ken tastes blood in his mouth.

Ken's four front teeth staple the centre of his lips together. His lips open near the corners of his mouth and turn upward, not down, against the restraint of the central incisor quartet. Ken closes his eyes and turns his head slightly towards the hollow below his right collarbone. His whole collarbone moves up and down, makes Ken's head move like one of those little plaster football player dolls with big helmet heads that bobble atop a wire spring neck.

Mumma can hear Ken's almost silent laughter, his breath exiting his nose in quiet bundles of five little snorts.

Ken, Mumma thinks, as a tear rolls down his right cheek and splashes on the tile floor entrance hall, you drop that sofa on my new floor and I swear I'll smack you 'til Sunday.

C'mon, she curls thought waves into the roots of his hair, Buck up, Ken. This can't be the only time someone else has noticed — Mumma's eyes dart to the other end of the sofa, Larry — Larry's bee-oh. You're a professional, Man. Don't drop that sofa.

"Penelope Jean." Pen's sensors scramble, then decode high alert paralysis. Mumma's pointer finger says shhhhhhh. Pen detects the crinkle fans. Mumma opens crinkle fans beside her eyes when she is pretendnice — butbeingmean to Pen in public or when there are other people in the house. Mumma slowly moves her shhhhhhh finger ninety degrees downward, points at Pen.

Pen's eyes say, "Not right now, I'm busy," to the tip of Mumma's finger. The crinkle fans and Mumma's jumbo flaring chocolate chips say, "Pen, stop trying to find the Turrible or something turrible will happen to you." Pen unhooks her thumbs from her suspenders, and runs through the dining room into the kitchen. "Don't point Mumma, it's not nice," she hollers and runs down the back steps, out the back door to look for other Turribles.

"Centre it against the far wall, please. And a good six inches away from the wall, too."

Mumma knows Wing will move the sofa sometime in the night, but she wants the room to look settled, completed, for herself. Mumma wraps her left arm under her brassiere, her right hand over her mouth, Mumma's index finger, a beauty pageant sash pressing across the torso of her Miss Congeniality nose. That is a turrible smell, she thinks, as she feigns the bemusement of the woman wearing a tailored housedress (with darts!) in the Endust ad in last week's *Woman's Day*. The Endust woman, because of her now dust-free furniture, so suddenly beset with waxy fresh life and huge gooping wads of time, contentment, possibility, that woman can pause during the day, eyes turned Heavenly, thank you God for aerosol dusting aids, to have celestial thoughts of delightful things to do with, for, and to her family: mother-daughter matching outfits, park picnics, and Junior Miss Klondike Days pageants.

"That looks right," Mumma says, as Ken adjusts the front corner of the sofa, unpockets eight rug-covered coasters from his coverall pocket and hands three to Larry.

Although Wing brings home the bread, and fruit and veg, and Silverwood's Dairy delivers, Mumma shops for everything else. What a lot of nonsense, Mumma thinks, flipping through *Woman's Day* while queued at the supermarket last week. No sense at all. Look at that Endust woman's hair, that's not a home perm, that hair hires someone else to do the dusting; and whose Aunt Fanny wears, hmmh, looks like a girdle and leather pumps to dust furniture; a housedress with glossy black buttons, a topstitched collar, and darts! — really; but most of all, girdle or no girdle, don't stand there and tell me those hips have taken even one tour of duty through the straits of childbearing. At the checkout stands, the kids play ooow canIhava. Mumma flips through the magazines, plays what's wrong with this picture. [Note: About thirty-three years from now, Mumma will find Waldo in her grandson's books with uncanny speed, "Here, and here, there, there he is again," and will make perceptive, albeit not always appropriate comments about the wearing of a bobble hat and a red-and-white striped sweater in the myriad of contexts in which she finds the hero.]

"There's a coffee shop a couple of blocks away," Ken says, "I think we'll take our lunch now. We'll be gone about forty minutes, it's not on the clock." Ken presses the middle joint of his curved finger against the end of his nose, moves his finger in enthusiastic little circles, as if to massage the cartilage, scratch an inside itch. "Kind of warm in here. Nice warm day, you might want to open the windows."

Mumma's head becomes the helmeted football dolly head, the wire-spring neck relaxing, she nods her head, little shakes of agreement.

Wing takes a Red Delicious apple from the wooden crate, gently rubs off the shavings from the excelsior nest, and polishes the fruit in a clean white cloth. Turning the apple to its best side, Wing gently wedges the apple in place, one fruit brick in a magnificent red apple pyramid under construction.

The front door of Maple Leaf Grocery and Confectionary has a display window on each side. The floor plates in each display case slope downward towards the window, and Wing has a series of different-coloured display boards and risers. Wing proceeds as quickly as the task allows, a keen bit of physics to keep the apples from rolling forward and bruising against the window.

Only a landmark in downtown Edmonton because it marks a location that is due west of the Main Post Office building, Wing opens the store on Rice Street at 8:00 in the morning on weekdays, just as he puts the finishing touches on his window displays.

The red apple pyramid is twinned by an identical pyramid of Red Delicious apples in the other display window. Wing's royal blue display boards, which cover the floor plates of the two display cases, make the pyramids appear to rise out of water. In the right foreground of the other display window, near the window, Wing has set a program from the Edmonton Light Opera production of *The Magic Flute*, four inches back from the window. A gentleman's evening scarf, cream silk damask, rests at an angle, carefully folded, on the bottom right corner of the program. The bottom of a silver cigarette case on top of the scarf runs parallel to the bottom of the opera program. Wing has combed the fine corded silk fringe of the scarf flat and even.

Wing fingers through the excelsior, looking for the top apple. In this display window, Wing has left a black leather evening bag with a rhinestone clip standing and open. Wing placed white evening gloves in the palm of his hand and tossed them gently across the opening of the purse, leaving the clip visible. The glove on top twisted slightly, opened the small slit than runs between the wrist and forearm. Exquisite button loops form a white scallop edge along one side of the opening. The pearlized buttons on the other side shine coldly, even in shadow.

The Monday morning sun on his shoulder blades feels hot as Wing paces along the sidewalk to look at the window displays. Hullo Joe, Wing's raised palm says to Joe Heinz, the chicken man next door. The shhshhshh of the corn husk broom stops under the awning for Heinz Poultry and Meat, the flick of Joe's wrist says, Hullo Wing.

Wing hooks his thumbs at the front of his waist, wraps his hands around the small of his back. The window frieze, bronze-coloured, black-outlined lettering to "Maple Leaf Grocery and Confectionary," wraps at Wing's eye level in both windows. In each window, the top three rows of apples in the pyramids are visible just above the lettering. The apex of each pyramid rises out of "y" in "Grocery." Wing moves his shoulder blades away from each other to stretch his back, and walks back into the store.

At the close of Monday's business, 4:45 p.m., Ralph Goodwin, Barrister and Solicitor, leaves his office, last to leave locks the door, as a point of pride, Ralph Goodwin has locked the door every day for the past ten years. He crosses Rice Street from the McLeod Block to retrieve his opera program and gear, and the evening gloves and bag belonging to "the Missus." [Note: Over thirty-five years from now, after Judy LaMarsh, after the sexual revolution, after *Ms.* magazine and Baby x, after equal pay for equal work, after the Canadian workplace culture adopts Take Your Daughter to Work Day, after the Canadian Charter of Rights and Freedoms, Lizzie will be speaking to an old high school classmate, a medium-young turk with the law firm Goodwin Evans, and he will tell her that he and "the Wife" just joined the Royal Glenora Club to play tennis in winter — "the Wife"!]

Ralph has stood at his office window all day long, watching the secretaries and downtown workers, his partners even, stopping in front of the Maple Leaf and coming out of the store moments later munching an apple and carrying a brown paper bag. [Note: One of those workers, Stanley Short, young architect, a young turk before anyone thought to call budding young professional men young turks, had the fortune to come early, to see the twin apple pyramids, and sixteen years later, reminiscing and eating an apple after a lunchtime workout at the downtown YMCA, may have become, without his even knowing, the critical tipping catalyst to the design of a nature conservatory in Edmonton's river valley.]

Ralph cast aside the entire billable day, ditched every single one of the ten six-minute segments in every blessed hour, door closed, please hold my calls, to watch the pyramids racing with each other to extinction. The pace of sales heightened as the apples descended in their display. Ralph could learn a thing or two from his food-stylist neighbour across the street about creating interest. And Wing could learn a thing or two from his lawyer neighbour across the street about the almighty hour, and how to monetize time.

"Wing, you are one crazy guy who sure knows how to sell a piece of fruit," Ralph says, clapping Wing on the shoulder, and pulling a five-dollar bill from his wallet. "I guess you win this one." The empty blue window displays look post-party. Wing wins most of the time, but usually just a cup of coffee. Today, Ralph wins too, quietly amused at seeing his and the Missus's ordinary fancy belongings in extraordinary settings, secretly thrilled at the public display in broad daylight anonymity.

"Thanks for the loan of the stuff, Ralph," Wing says, taking the bill from Ralph's middle and index fingers, and handing him a clean cardboard flat containing the opera gear, "And here's a bag of apples for Missus Goodwin."

"Hey, you didn't cheat me, did you? You sold all the ones in the window, right?" Ralph is simultaneously embarrassed to have made the accusation and skeptical about losing.

"No cheating. I got these apples from the box in the cold room, not from the window. Still nice and cold," Wing says, thinking Ralph still believes that the only reason he can lose to me is if I cheat. Wing wonders if Ralph's heart's as visible on his sleeve to anyone else, when Wing can see it across Rice Street through a window high up on the sixth floor.

Wing doesn't intend to be a food stylist, Wing Lee, the accidental aesthete. Wing's displays, his Dominion Day cherry tomato and cauliflower new Canadian flags, his back-to-school acorn squash bells, the simple black cloth draping and pooling over the picture frame set on a table for Remembrance Day, the Maple Leaf windows figure frequently as game pieces in the chit-chat of downtown Edmonton. And although he graciously accepts his customers' compliments, and although Ralph is partially right, Wing does know how to sell a piece of fruit, what Wing Lee has a real passion for is a sense of order, everything having a place.

Everything. Just put it in its place. Rows of apples in boxes look tidy, but not in place, today. Today, they should be stacked upon each other in pyramids. The ones left in the box, make one or two small pyramids in the box, don't leave them in rows. Next month, or week, or day, many varieties of apples are placed in multi-coloured chevron bands. After that, lift the boxes into the windows, the rows of apples in boxes are right in place.

It doesn't stop with apples. For Wing, every single thing has a place. Wing doesn't insist that doing his thing becomes Mumma's thing, or anyone else's thing, Wing's composition of place a solo act. Mumma tries to keep the furniture minimal and the clutter non-existent on the home front, a gesture of support and understanding she extends to her hard-working husband. Mumma understands it is hard to move furniture at night with no lights on, at night when everyone else should be asleep, when Mumma pretends to sleep. At an early age, the kids learn to weave around the morning's new furniture configurations.

Wing tags everything with the date of acquisition, with the price paid (if purchased), and any other pertinent details, such as gifted from whom, or from what store or city or vacation. Wing's calligraphy is small and exact, his ink indelible. Sometimes he counts the number of Lees in the phone book, a neatly scribed marginalia, "53." Every so often, Wing will bring the bathroom scale and yardstick to the kitchen, line the kids up, and make a permanent lined paper record of their heights and weights pinned down by black triangular points onto the black pages of the photo album with a date of record, say, 17/09/60 — but not always with a photo.

Mumma refuses to be measured. Early in their relationship, Mumma learns to put things behind cupboard doors, into drawers, closets, anywhere away, a gesture of support and understanding she extends to herself — visitors, even family, do not need to know that the cold cream in the bathroom has a recorded birthday or homecoming, now two months old, and was bought on sale for $1.29. [Note: Mumma and Wing never realize how the jumbled conversations, the relentless labelling and the bringing home of new baby siblings may have affected their children. As a preschooler, Tom will close the bathroom door and no one else will know that he will get an ache behind his navel, an ache in the shape of a toilet paper roll, twenty-five minutes of pulling and prying, looking for 24/05/57, or 6 lbs. 8 oz., or Royal Alex, anything, on the inner folds of his innie. Years later, at university, Pen will spin an intimate, compelling and totally fallacious fable of a culturally-based ritual, the Chinese baby tattoo. Five times as foreplay, four times not all the way, twenty-year old Pen will dare the boys to find her birthmark tattoo.]

A tiny plastic and metal license plate-like tablet suspended from a short length of ball chain jingles against the ring of keys as Wing turns a key in the deadbolt on the front door of the Maple Leaf. Holding all the keys in his fingers, Wing jiggles the ring to move the tablet like a pendulum. Aluminum on one side, the other side displays a series of black letters on a yellow background, covered by a hard, clear plastic window. A thin rolled edge of aluminum running along the border keeps the plastic in place. Wing thinks about summer vacation, Key Number 6F, Chickadee Bungalows. The gold embossed lettering on the leather key toggle: "If you find this key, please drop it in any mailbox, to be returned to Chickadee Bungalows, Box 16, General Delivery, Banff, Alberta. Thanks!" Now there's a place for a vacation, Wing thinks.

The tablet swings back and forth in front of Wing's nodding head. The engraving on the back of the aluminum tablet promises that these keys too should be dropped in any mailbox if they are lost and found — then, The War Amps will relocate them to their proper place. Wing knows a lot of Vets, a lot of his customers are Vets, but no War Amps. And while Wing doesn't know a War Amp or anyone with anything amputated, and has never misplaced his keys, his keys never dropped in the mailbox by a good Samaritan, mailed to the War Amps and then sent back to Wing, how can you not support such a worthy cause, caring for people, putting keys back where they belong?

....

Mumma opens the little window in the bathroom; that turrible smell all over the New House has dissipated somewhat, but one more bit of cross ventilation won't hurt. Mumma examines the sky above The New House and thinks of Katiya, her neighbour at the Old House, how they visited while each tended her own garden, the ease of slipping on Wing's gardening shoes to pull a few green onions for dinner, the little piece of green glass in the stucco by the back door that was from a green bottle of 7-Up, the other little piece of green glass with the smaller red label reading "7-Up." One nice thing about this house — not only could the Old House fit into the hip pocket of the New House, the New House has lots of drawers. And Mumma hears Pen open and shut, one, two, "eighteen, Mumma," eighteen copper handles, one on each of the doors of the built-in cupboards.

Mumma recalls Wing saying as the two of them were packing their parfait glasses for the move, cold desserts being in vogue when they married, "Mumma, I think the New House feels like it's just the place for us." Maybe Wing's right. Mumma wonders, Oh wow, what will Lizzie think of the New House when she comes home from piano camp later that week?

Pen proclaims herself the Queen of Mudlandia, and all its lands as far as she can see — the back lane which is not gravelled yet, behind the garage where Mumma says the vegetable garden will go, the pristine kidney-shaped concrete back patio, and the vast yard beside the garage. The air smells like wet leaves and absolute power. The loyal subjects arrayed before her fit the bill for the type every despotic ruler desires: quiet, cowed and ready to obey. Well, the loyal subject, yes actually, just one subject. Jane has not grown out of her afternoon nap, still napping inside with Mumma, who took the opportunity to change into more comfortable clothes after the movers finished. Tom stands in front of Pen, his brown irises tipped up to the top halves of his eyes. Pen frowns, disgusted with his red stupid cheeks and his mucousy boogery nose.

"Why can't I be King?" Tom whines.

Right, Pen thinks, Booger King, "Because, you're my brother, and I can't marry you."

"But. Well, okay, but why do you get to be Queen?"

"Because I'm the oldest. Ah-duh."

"But. Well, okay, but why can't I be The Prince then?"

"Tell you what," Pen considers Tom for a moment then says, "you can be the Prince and the White Knight and the Innkeeper and the school boy —"

"Really?"

"But you also have to be my slave."

"Nnnohh."

"That's the deal."

"Okay."

"Can I play?"

Pen turns in the direction of the voice coming from a blonde ringleted girl, her size, standing on their patio, wearing a purple ski jacket, white turtleneck and tights, a pink tulle tutu, and the same rubber boots as Pen and Tom. Before Pen can close her mouth, before she can find and pull the words through her vocal chords to speak, tires squealing on new cement, a loud blunt impact, the sound of a couple of hard but not heavy things falling on metal, and a resoundingly muttered "Well gawddammit," stop all action.

"That will be my mother," the girl in the pink tulle tutu says, turning on her heels slowly, "I'm Bonnie. I gotta go home now."

Pen and Tom turn to read each other's faces and without saying a word, they follow the path that Bonnie has taken down the lane. Mumma follows shortly behind them, the back screen door banging, a waking-up Jane bundled up in a sweater in Mumma's arms. Curiosity bells Mumma and her kids, each of them drawn to the site of what the heck was that.

What Mumma notices first is not that the lovely turquoise and ivory Thunderbird is sideways in the large single car garage, but that she has never before looked through a garage door and seen the profile of a person in the driver's seat. A long-handled spade, teetering on the passenger side of the hood, rolls off and echoes on the garage floor. The driver's side window is rolled all the way down, and the driver, a woman with a turquoise silk scarf tied over her blonde hair, holds onto the steering wheel with both hands, and moves her index fingers as if trying to remember what gear will get the car turned around and parked in the usual manner. Bonnie smiles and waves at the kids as they walk towards her on the driveway.

"Are you all right?" Mumma asks, approaching the garage slowly. Mumma takes a surreptitious glance down at herself beyond Jane's pant legs and and stockinged feet, and feels the internal pilot light fire up her heating element; such an old housedress, and she pulled on what was at the back door without thinking, rubber boots, now covered with mud, and dirtying the driveway of her new neighbour.

The car door opens and two rubber boots swing out onto the pavement. "Those gawddamn idiots at the hardware think they're God, think they know everything about matching paint chips, they know what's best, stupid, stupid buggers. I'm fine, thanks. Just embarrassed. Pride's a little damaged, but nothing else that matters. Don't suppose you know how to drive standard do you — I'm Bonnie's mom — not that I suppose that's going to help much. This is my daughter Bonnie, I'm Sally. You must be the new folks on the block. What about all this muck, eh?"

When Wing pulls up the driveway, his eyes scan the new back-yard and he feels his chest tighten. Wing slowly reaches behind the steering wheel, and shifts into park in front of the empty garage on the driveway. The War Amps tag swings gently below the ignition as Wing turns off the car, but Wing doesn't take the key out immediately. He rolls the side window down, as if it were the glass wildly distorting the image.

Rubber boots. Three of them. Stuck past their soles in mud in the middle of the back yard. Three child-size rubber boots, Wing concludes, a pair and an odd. The mud backyard looks like a track-and-field meet has been held on it, hundreds of footprints, ruts, and ball-sized craters, but Wing expects this. He doesn't even notice the mucky footprints all over the back patio. It's the odd boot that's very much out of place. That, and the pair of boots posed neatly together, as if a small invisible marching soldier stands in them, at ease.

Wing stands on the back patio, studying the boots for a few minutes. He uncrates a cigarette from a pack in his suit jacket pocket, and cupping his hand around the flame of his lighter, lights a cigarette. By all appearances, a man enjoying a late afternoon cigarette in the perfect quiet of his backyard until the back screen door slams.

"Daddy Daddy the furniture came the furniture came and we played outside in the mud and I have a new friend and her name is Bonnie and one of the moving men stunk and Mumma says that you're not supposed to tell someone that they stink even if they stink and Tom and I and Bonnie played outside and then Bonnie had to go home and Tom and I played school way out in the backyard but Tom got stuck in the mud and I got stuck too and Tom starts crying and I say 'Don't be such a baby' and he cries harder and I say 'Crybaby what's the matter with you' and he sucks air like he goes phup-phup-phup-phup like he can't talk cause he's been crying so hard and so I pinch him and he says 'Don't I'm stuck' and so I say 'You're not stuck Stupid it's just your boots walk out of them' and he says 'I'm stuck' like he's given up so I walk out of my boots and then I run to the patio and Stupid cries louder again so then I run back out to him and I pull him out of his boots but one of them stays on his foot and he loses his other sock and I drag him back to the patio and Mumma yells out the window 'What are you doing to Tom?' so I go back again in my socks and I get his sock Bonnie's mom can drive sideways and do I get anything for saving Tom?"

....

"It's too bad your brother's sick, because if there's no prince, there's no point," Bonnie says, "What should we do?"

"Well, do you wanna play school?"

"Nah, my Mom says the school's going to open next week. You could come over and see my stuff, but my mom said I should play over here today. What d'you got there?"

"Try one. My Mumma gave one of these to Tom and then she put them in her underwear drawer. They're called baby Aspirin, cause they're little and pink like babies. Chew it."

"Mmmmm. They're kinda good."

"I know. But you can only have two a day, that's what Tom gets. It's medi-sin."

"Oh."

"What are we going to do?"

"Have you met Michelle, yet?" Bonnie asks.

"No."

"She's bossy, but she's got chalk."

"Okay."

"Too bad your brother's sick."

"Yeah."

Mumma checks the DeVilbiss vaporizer in Tom's room and dabs a bit more Vicks VapoRub in the cup on top. [Note: Tom will call the vaporizer DevilBiss, a permanent fixture in his childhood bedroom. An asthmatic, and the only one in the family, when Tom is an old man and Mumma even older, she will draw a straight line between Tom's inhaler and Dad, the smoker, picking up Tom and carrying him everywhere when he was a baby, which Dad did not do with the girls.] She feels his cheek, and tucks his arm under the flannel sheet. Too bad that Tom's feeling sick, a chesty cough and cold. Mumma's mind keeps returning to her new neighbour Sally Faber, Sal, the sideways parker. Her husband has had to Call-in-a-Favour with Walt McBean of McBean's Lumber. Today, Walt's going to send out the big truck with the winch and dollies to try to get Sally's car out of the garage and Walt says it's going to be nip and tuck. What are winch and dollies? Mumma wants to be there to take in the proceedings, but a sick kid lassoes Mumma, keeps her close to home, and closer to a more sub-dued version of herself. Still, that nip and tuck makes Mumma wild with the need to know.

....

Winch and dollies. Wing tries not to think of that sideways car, as if it is possible to forget. Neighbour seems to be a funny guy,

"I told her she could have the garage for her car. Wasn't even going to be home for a few hours, but she still wants to race me for it," Don Faber winked his eye at his new neighbours, "Yeah, just kidding Sal!" What is body language if not rhetorical, Wing and Mumma blushed red last night and a very small bit later, went home.

Well, Wing can do something about the other. Wing lays out three small pieces of cardboard, cut to the size of business cards. Before him lie three rectangular plastic sleeves with brass safety pins in their backs that Ralph Goodwin brought over at morning coffee. "Sure, I know what you mean, Wing, I've got some in my desk, you're welcome to them. You're going to use them in a display are you? No? Ohhh, Bartlett pears today, okay, the usual time."

Under Wing's supervision, each of his kids will fill volumes of penmanship books, at home, before they reach the age of nine. No surprise then that Wing's design and execution of lettering has a stencil-like consistency and precision, the letters placed carefully on pencilled-in straight lines and each line exactly centred. After the ink has completely dried, Wing carefully erases the pencil lines.

Each plastic sleeve has a small flap that snaps over the back and runs along the top length of the sleeve, making a rectangular badge. Wing opens the flap on each sleeve and inserts one of the cards. He lines them up in a row across the top of his desk blotter. At the back of the Maple Leaf Grocery and Confectionary, an old wooden office table with a gooseneck lamp and desk blotter constitutes the office.

....

For a new grocery store, you'd think the carts would be in better shape, Mumma thinks, then realizes that what's out of alignment is her driving and not the cart. Mumma suddenly recognizes that the problem has never been the carts, but in the new grocery store, Mumma takes notice for the first time. With Jane in the baby seat, and Tom and Pen pushing and pulling at her hips and the cart, Mumma's entourage-driven grocery cart moves like a bumper car in between the aisles.

But the store by the Old House where Mumma never cared how the carts steered and knew where to find everything has impossible math: two buses away multiplied by three kids. Home, home, new electric range, the discouraging word here being Endust. Some of the women in this store look like they actually do wear the girdle, the leather pumps and the fancy housedresses (with darts!) to dust their furniture. She smiles at them and says, "Hello," and they smile back, "Hello."

"Here, let Mumma put these in her purse. Pen, where's yours?"

"I dunno. I guess I lost it."

Mumma quickly unpins the plastic badges from Tom and Jane's tee-shirts. Two little pin prick holes appear over their hearts. She pricks her finger on one of the badge pins, reads the four lines: "Tom Lee, 13918 Summit Place, Edmonton, HU8-3152."

"It's not so they won't get lost, Mumma," Wing said this morning, the plastic badges appearing on the breakfast table, one at each of the kid's place settings. "It never even occurred to me that they would ever be lost. Or missing. But it's a New House and it's their place and that's where they belong and this way, they'll know."

Not today, Mumma thinks, the snik on the clasp of her purse an indisputable confirmation.

Pen feels the round nubby of the garter holding up Mumma's stocking, rubs the fabric of Mumma's dress and feels the elastic armour Mumma calls her girl. Pen's sensors are on high alert when she sees Michelle's mom quickly walk up to them.

"Hello, you must be Pen's mom. I'm Michelle's mom, Monique, Monique Oliver. I'm a little distracted, have you seen a little Mountie in the store, about this tall?" Mrs. Oliver's hand levels at just above her waist.

"A little what?"

"A little Mountie. Sometimes we dress Trevor up like a little Mountie when we're going out, little red serge jacket and blue pants, brown hat with a wide brim and whistle. I don't like those leather harnesses, and he's a runner. Have you seen him? One minute he's right here, the next he's gone. Like now."

"Oh. No, I haven't seen him. I'm sorry. I'll keep an eye out."

Pen flattens her body against the white and chrome frozen food chest.

"Well, he'll show, he always does, but it still makes me anxious. At least this way, we can usually find him pretty fast. Love to visit, but got to find my little man." [Note: The little man will run through many family vacations before he outgrows the uniform and Trevor Oliver, Senior, will make a killing in "let me give you something for the little fella"-s. After all, who doesn't want their picture taken with a Mountie, at Yellowstone National Park, Jasper National Park, Niagara Falls, and Anaheim, California. In Jasper, a souvenir photo with the little Mountie will become almost as ubiquitous as the postcard, "Black bear on its hind legs leaning into the cab of the red truck." Trevor Oliver, Junior, will stop running, slow down, and become a park warden for a national park in the Rockies, not Jasper.]

Pen tries to put her arm around her mother's waist. Mumma has her going-out smell. When Pen was little, the smell of face powder always made her sad and Mumma cheerful. But I'm here, Pen thinks, and Tom and Jane, out with Mumma and her face powder smell, all of us together, so why does Mumma seem so tucked up inside herself?

Pen knows how to cheer up Mumma, get some happy colour behind that face powder. With the milk man delivering milk and cream, and Dad bringing home fruit and vegetables from the store, and bread from Alberta Bakery, Mumma only ever comes to a place like this to get meat, Mumma not caring about sprinkles, or birthday cake ballerina candle holders, or those delicious-looking lollipops shaped like tiny balls and tied together like little colourful balloons with an elastic band.

"Mumma," Pen exclaims in a timbre and volume reminiscent of a sideways driver careening into a single-car garage, "Mumma," in a voice loud and clear enough to make everyone on the aisle look up. "Look at all the Meat. Hooole-ly. Oh Mumma, Could We have some? Huh? Could We? Can We Please try some Meat? Oh please, Please Mumma, Mumma can We buy some Meat?" [Note: Jane is the only one of the kids who doesn't refuse to wear Wing's name badge, at least until she starts school, which gives a very pleased Wing too many years to make a ridiculous number of Jane badges. "If you ever do get lost, someone will know exactly where you belong, where to bring you back," he tells Jane quietly. Learning how the war amps tags on Dad's keychain work, and remembering at least a couple of the family summer trips to Chickadee Bungalows before she started school, several decades after wearing her last Jane badge, Jane still will cross the street to avoid walking in front of a mailbox.]

Number 188. "Peeking" Duck

"**Is your house all clean?** It's New Year's Eve, you know."

Hello, Pig Pen. Peace Assassin. Joy Molester.

That's what Jane thinks, those are the words stuck against the fine mesh filter lodged between Jane's mind and her mouth. Banal words flow through the fine mesh, right past the pejorative nicknames and other detritus trapped there.

"Oh. Is it Chinese New Year? I completely forgot."

"Well, you've got about three hours before midnight your time. I'm just getting ready for bed, here."

Right. Three hours. Jane inventories just the clutter in the kitchen: Piles of articles torn from magazines that Leo wants for future reference; a shopping bag full of never-tried recipes, clipped from the Sunday paper. Three dozen or so miniature pots and cooking tools, stacked beside the stove, to be hung in a three-dimensional wall frieze. Two boxes of received and opened Christmas presents that haven't moved since Christmas. A pile of junk mail waiting to be recycled.

Like all the rooms in their house. Three hours will not tidy the house Jane describes as a two-storey purse with five appliances and a deadbolt. She knows it, and so does her sister Pen. Jane forgot about Chinese New Year. Jane's focused on what to give up for Lent.

Jane asks, "So what's the new year coming up? Is it Ferret? Iguana? Year of the Miniature Donkey?" Not bunnies, not that small, Jane now thinking about the dust ponies nickering in her study.

"Year of the Tiger, dumbass. I've had my bath and washed my hair. Tomorrow, I'm having people over for New Year's dinner and I've also volunteered to make pancakes for school."

"Pancakes? Oh, right, Pancake Tuesday's tomorrow."

The Jane filter snares Shrove Tuesday in a public school? And, Pancakes cooked by a Helicopter Chef.

Jane swirls a piece of ice around the wall of her highball glass, as Pen describes the dishes she will prepare for her dinner guests.

"I phoned Mumma to find out how to steam a whole fish," Pen laughs. "She was so mad that I called long distance for that. Of course you should know that traditionally, people serve fish for Chinese New Year's, has to be a whole fish. Turns out I don't have a pan large enough. I suppose I could wrap it in parchment and bake it in the oven. Or nuke pieces in the microwave..."

That's uber traditional, Jane thinks, and then chides herself, "I thought you said the fish had to be whol —"

"Wait a minute," Pen interrupts, "I have that fabulous stainless steel fish poacher I've never used. Oh my gosh, I forgot about that. Great, that's what I'll do."

As Pen continues to describe her party menu, the Jane filter becomes clogged with woody broccoli and rubbery red pepper strips, chicken balls, crab and cream cheese wrapped in wonton wrappers, the whole mess covered in shiny thick sauce, the colour of a neon light. The pancakes and the words, Pig Pen, drown in congealing authentic ersatz Chinese cuisine.

Chinese New Year's Eve. Jane feels a skiff of acid lightly coat the roof of her mouth — in a familial frenzy of end-of-the-year housecleaning, grade school Jane throws up after polishing the piano with aerosol furniture polish. The day before Chinese New Year's Eve, the annual cleaning everything that wouldn't move, and bathing everyone that would.

"What will Leo and I have tomorrow? Same as tonight, I suppose, leftover pasta with a salad," says Jane. "I completely forgot."

"Leftover pasta and a salad?" Pen laughs, "You kill me."

No, You kill me, Jane thinks, Gut me like a fish.

Every year, the rules change. First, Mumma says, you can't take a bath or wash your hair all day New Year's Day, or you'll wash away your good luck. Your house should be clean and tidy, and all your debts settled. You shouldn't do any housework on the actual day, just stay at home with your family and try not to annoy each other too much. But one year, when smoky, beer-smelling Pen comes home from a date after midnight, the rule bends: you can shower on New Year's Eve, even if it's past midnight and into New Year's day, as long as you haven't gone to bed yet. Then, there's the Eddie and

Betty exception. When good friends, like Eddie and Betty Fein-Lo have a house party New Year's Day and don't know any better, especially when Eddie's brother from Vancouver plans on bringing fresh prawns with him, iced in a Styrofoam cooler, you can go to their house, be modern and enjoy their prawns-in-winter hospitality. The rules change once more when Mumma finds out that Tom has been carrying a balance on his credit card.

"Mumma, how can there be an exception for credit card balances?"

When Jane confronts Mumma about how the rules always change, Mumma shrugs, "There isn't a book. It's just what I hear. You know. Different horses, different mouths."

Jane has her own rules for Chinese New Year. It's the one day of the year she doesn't beat herself up for living at the bottom of a giant purse. Then, any New Year's resolution that she had for the first of January she resurrects, fresh starts, the intervening period just a dress rehearsal. She also has an extra long and vigorous shower first thing in the morning, quite willing to risk washing her luck down the drain, if it means the chance to change her luck from bad to good.

"Pen, I guess my house will be the same as always," Jane concedes.

"It sure the hell will be, with that attitude. You've got to step up. No wonder all the great cultural traditions in the world are fading." The Jane filter catches, Like getting stoned in the West stairwell during study period in high school, Pen, that great tradition? And, So I'm on the hook personally for the crumbling of civilization because I've got stuff and a messy house. I like my stuff.

"If you were a mother, you'd get your act together. Like you'd have a choice. You're not a baby anymore. Still need Mumma to bail you out? Grow up. Step up and get that damn house of yours organized. Look, I'm bringing the twins out this summer, you've got five months, and we'll want to come visit on our way to the mountains."

The telephone receiver transmits, blah, blah, sixteen to twenty for dinner blah, blah, sugar snap peas, blah, blah, promised to take the girls skating after school, blah, blah, will have to change the whole menu. Jane swirls her glass and thinks, what's the secret Melting Ice Cube, why are you having more fun than me?

Pen annihilates the potential for any domestic disaster. She keeps her house, her life, and the twins highly organized. Jane pictures her sister giving each of the girls filing cabinets in the womb. File the man Stanley under D for daddy, cross-reference to mommy's file H for husband.

"And because I've volunteered to cook pancakes at the school, I'm going to smell like pancakes all day long," Pen whines.

Jane mouths, "Not after you've cooked fish," then wonders whether that was out loud.

"Very funny." Pen's voice heats the blood in Jane's face.

Oh well, Jane thinks, there's bound to be errant outflow on a high volume day.

The phone's ear piece radiates heat into Jane's ear. Gotta go, blah, blah, Happy New Year, Jane hangs up the phone.

Quintessential Pen, that conversation. Jane tips her glass to lick the last drops of watery scotch from the nub of ice resting against her lip and the rim of the upturned glass. In Jane's mind, Pen strives for and achieves perfect geometry — Pen's double-pointed life stylus grounded at the exact point where she is at, the other end of the compass imbedded where she wants to be, Pen measures and draws the straightest line between the two points. She travels light and fast, keeping the line taut. Nothing gets in her way. Jane still feels the poke of Pen's finger through the telephone, jabbing her repeatedly in the arm, get that, get that?

"Hi Mumma, it's me, Jane."

"Janie, what's up? Why are you calling long distance?"

"Why didn't you tell me it was Chinese New Year tomorrow when I talked to you last night?"

"What do you mean, why didn't I tell you? Why didn't I tell you it was winter? Why didn't I tell you it was Christmas?"

"Well I didn't know."

"Hmmmm. Tomorrow is Chinese New Year."

"Thanks. Thanks, Mumma. You know that Pen. She phoned me, wanted to know if I was ready, was my house clean, what I was cooking, was it authentic Chinese New Year food, as if she knows. Drives me nuts."

"You're not trying to cook a fish are you?"

"No. Of course not."

"Good. Stinks up the whole house. So it's traditional, p-u. Just remember, don't do any housework on New Year's Day."

"Um-hmm."

"And don't try to clean up tonight either," Mumma cautions. When Leo and Jane took Mumma for a drive in the country the last time she visited them in Calgary, the foothills made Mumma think of the piles of books and clothes and trinky-fussy junk all over her daughter's house. How can Jane live that way, Mumma frowns, her baby who, to Mumma's dismay, is still a tattletale.

"Believe me, I won't."

"And none of this bitch-bitchy-crap talk either. Everything you do and think on New Year's Day is what's going to happen the rest of the year."

"I know. Hey Mumma, not to change the subject but, to change the subject, what are you giving up for Lent this year?"

"I don't know," Mumma says, "I think maybe lion taming, sabre dancing. Maybe horse jumping, I'll think of something." Rats, Mumma thinks, I thought she might forget to ask this year.

"I was thinking of giving up dog sledding this year."

"Oh, that's a good one. Maybe that's what I'll give up too. Lent right after Chinese New Year; that doesn't happen every year."

....

Mumma attended church every week, a regular church go-er before all her kids came. She taught Sunday school before she married Wing, met him at a Chinese United Church social function. Still, Mumma feels muddlish when it comes to church, and God. Mumma has tentatively concluded that something must get lost in translation. Not just something, though. Lots. For instance, although all the Ministers in the Chinese United Church take their studies in English, even if they intend to be good ministers, their English is often lacking; what if they're just lousy translators? That aside, what if some beliefs or actions don't translate, what if there aren't quite the right words and phrases for the basics: not the platitudes (which Mumma thinks can be lazy, false and often harmful shortcuts to careful, compassionate thinking), but ground floor essence. The problem of translation goes deeper than ministers who struggle with English, since English wasn't even one of the languages of biblical people. What about all the Bible translations, the different versions over history, let alone all the languages the Bible has been translated into all over the world, talk about different horses, different mouths. Why leave important stuff up to language skills, of all things, how does the real meaning sift out through multiple translations over eons, but when Mumma thinks about this, the muddle gets too deep. Oh wow. One good thing, though: the muddle motivates Mumma to be always on the lookout for inside information on how God works.

Just before Lent thirty-three years ago, Mumma's next door neighbour, Mrs. Eileen Walker, persuades Mumma to go on a diet with her. Mrs. Walker, raised Episcopalian in Colorado Springs, has only found a rough equivalency in the Anglican church in Edmonton but better than nothing, and definitely better than the other choices on the denominational menu. When Mumma asks, Eileen says yes, fatty foods definitely something worthy of giving up for Lent.

During a trip to the grocery store together, to look for diet-wise, non-fatty food for Lent, Mumma and Eileen agree that the contents of their grocery carts look very similar. Mumma does not mention the grocery stores in Chinatown where she does some of her shopping. Eileen does not mention her downtown trips to Eaton's food floor where she seeks and acquires comestibles not available in the average grocery store. That day, they take the long-course circuit, snaking through every aisle and then a perimeter search for perishables.

"Look, Mumma. Remember when the store ran out of food colouring last year to dye Easter eggs for church. Let's get some now." [Note: Eileen started calling her Mumma early on in their friendship. Although only five years younger than Mumma, when Eileen and her husband moved in next door, they had no children, and "knew not a soul" in Edmonton. Mumma and Wing and the kids became like family, and when Eileen asked if she could because she loved the idea of being part of a big family perpetually in motion, Mumma thought, Odd, but oh why not, everyone calls me Mumma.]

As they slip the cardboard sleeves filled with small glass bottles of Nutty Club food colouring into the carts, Mumma remembers how her cheeks ached, and that terrible taste of lips on egg shells, pricking little blow holes in the tops and bottoms, then blowing hard, expressing the liquid out of the shells of dozens of eggs. A few of the decorated eggs stayed home, but most were for the church. Many of those kids have parents occupied with daily survival, not the finer points of blowing out and dyeing Easter eggs. She thinks to remind Eileen of the rubber cheeks episode, then changes her mind. "Oh, I still have lots left from last year," Mumma says, struggling for a moment while she persuades the baby to let go, then returning the food colouring package to the shelf.

"This food colouring reminds me of a Palm Sunday when I was a teenager in Colorado Springs," Eileen says, moving her packets of sloppy joe mix to make room. "We had made all these palm leaves, big ones and little ones, but it was fairly humid and warm for that time of the year and the construction paper just limped right over. So some little genius bought all these cans of spray varnish. Stiffened up the paper, but the colour turned pretty vibrant, like this stuff. Mumma?"

Mumma's working a Kleenex from her purse, wiping cookie crumbs from Jane's mouth and hands, Jane trying to bat away every stroke with her free hand. Jane fiddles with the animal cracker box, almost figures out how to reopen the top, so Mumma slips it out of her hands and tosses the box into the cart. "I'm listening, Eileen."

"Well, even though we cracked a window open in the church basement, I think we got, you know, we got what the kids call high."

Jane starts to fuss, so Mumma retrieves the cookie box, and lays the string handle over the palm of Jane's dominant hand.

"One boy, Jeffrey Graham, he kept spraying the same leaf over and over. The next day we were all sick. Sick-sick-sick-sick-sick. Even by that Sunday, all the teenagers still looked a little gill-y, waving those palm leaves. Beautiful pageant though, by God, we Episcopalians from The Springs sure knew how to put on spectacular pageants — jeez, look at the price of butter."

They are still tut-tutting, those colour tablets in margarine boxes are pure poison, when Eileen stops in front of the upright dairy cooler with the glass door, filled with cottage cheese, sour cream, and aerosol whipping cream canisters.

"Mumma, what a blessing! Lord, this is such a good price for cottage cheese." Eileen shares her recipe for Flagpole Salad, which, she says, "is light and refreshing and appropriate for our program." She and Mumma check for the best dates on the tubs of cottage cheese while Jane holds onto the cookie box's string handle and thumps the animal crackers like a punching balloon.

....

Still small enough to fit in a high chair, Jane can almost feed herself. The other kids will come home from school for lunch in a few minutes. Mumma sets four place settings at the table, leaving Wing's place at the head of the table empty. Tom sits with Mumma, the two older girls on the other side, and Jane at the other end of the square table in the high chair. A bright green leaf of bibb lettuce lies on top of each plate, covered with a small mound of cottage cheese. Mumma has centred a ring of tinned pineapple on each cottage cheese serving. She busies herself cutting bananas in half, cross-wise, then peeling the skins off with the knife. She splits the maraschino cherries, and drains them in a little sieve. She recalls Eileen's instructions: place half a firm banana upright in the centre of the pineapple ring, top with half a maraschino cherry. Mumma takes the chopping board of prepared bananas to the table. Her fingertips gently grasp a banana half, and Jane watches Mumma turn her wrist as if Mumma's just discovered a banana for the first time, Mumma's mouth a perfect O. The banana doesn't fit, too large for the pineapple ring. With Jane as enthralled audience, Mumma's fingertips rotate the banana in little half-turn pushes, she snugly wedges the banana upright in the hole. Mumma's hands become a mask over the bottom half of her face, leaving only her bug eyes showing. She lowers the mask, reveals her tightly drawn fish lips. Mumma notices Jane mimicking her lips and eyes, so she deliberately relaxes her face by blinking and slowly moving her lower jaw in a sideways circle. Then, she picks up a shiny cherry half and gingerly places it on top of the banana. Hands flying, she becomes the masked Mumma once again, a high-pitched, breathy "oh" issues from behind the mask.

After washing their hands, the kids sit down to a leaf of lettuce, with a ring of canned pineapple half-submerged in a smeary blob of cottage cheese. Limp uneven coins of browning banana slices cover the entire surface of each plate. A bit of maraschino cherry juice bleeds pink into the curds of white cottage cheese in front of each kid. Their confused faces turn from their plates to each other, to their mother. The baby masticates the bottom half of a banana, the skin peeled back like a yellow gerbera daisy.

"Cottage cheese? Is someone on a diet?" Pen asks.

"Looks like something that's been in and come out again," Tom says, screwing up his mouth to seal the hatch.

"It's Lent, a special Lent meal," Mumma says, "special food, what God wants us to eat at this time of the year."

Pen takes a forkful of cottage cheese, "I don't think so. Tastes disgusting. Look at this," she says, the tines of her fork catch the edge of a browning banana slice.

Mumma has tasted it. It is disgusting. Other than milk and the very occasional piece of cheddar cheese, dairy products do not figure large in the family diet. Mumma's fingers interlace her left and right hands together in a ball as she leans her elbows against the table. Exactly thirty-seven minutes until the afternoon bell rings at school.

"Fine. There's some leftover chicken in the fridge. But eat the fruit."

"Hey, look at the baby." Tom has moved his plate to the tray on the Jane's high chair, and Jane takes a handful of cottage cheese and swallows slightly more than she throws on the floor.

The leaves of bibb lettuce make for a relatively quick clean up. As they run out the door, Mumma gives each kid a nickel to buy Life Savers after school.

"I thought I'd prepared a special Episcopalian Lent lunch."

"Oh God no. Mumma, a Lent lunch? Now where would you get an idea like that? It's just cottage cheese with a bit of fruit. Very light and refreshing."

"It's, you know...it's Naughty."

"What do you mean, 'naughty'? Can't be. I improvised it from a Campbell Kids children's book, recipes for Cream of Tomato Soup and Flagpole Salad."

"Eileen," Mumma leans on her kitchen table towards her neighbour who sips quietly from a steaming mug of coffee, "The banana and a pineapple ring? The cherry?"

"Oh, tch. You're being silly." Eileen frowns, and twirls her coffee spoon in her mug. "A lot of people eat cottage cheese when they're dieting."

Wherever would Mumma get the idea that Episcopalians eat naughty food for Lent? Naughty? Eileen pokes the tip of her spoon at the creamy mocha ellipse on the surface of the coffee.

Dieting, Mumma wonders, did she say dieting or dying?

For a while, hot liquid being slowly drawn through lips to the curved pool of a wordless tongue produces the only sound in the kitchen.

Mumma never brings up the subject of Lent with anyone else. She hears the minister say in a sermon that the Chinese United Church, and the United Church of Canada do not make a practice of Lent observance, if that's actually true. And none of the kids ever brings up Lent in conversations with Mumma. Except Jane. Jane remembers nothing of flagpole salad or cottage cheese for lunch, but every single year since she was eight (God knows where Jane heard about Lent), Jane desperately wants to and does discuss with Mumma giving up something for Lent. She's relentless. Mumma, she'll say, what should the two of us give up for Lent?

Mumma wonders whether Jane harbours creepy baby brain memory, God's way of punishing Mumma, the infant eavesdropping on her conversations with Eileen Walker and watching her mother's naughty lunch preparation. In the first few years, Mumma found Jane's little tradition kind of instructive. Jane and Mumma gave up things like candy, potato chips, soda pop. But as Jane grew older, Mumma feels the tradition became silly and mischievous, no, Mumma edits herself, the tradition became oddly ungodly, Jane proposing that they give up strange things like wrestling in warm jello, chasing greased pigs, hot shaving musclemen in tiny Speedos at the beach, wearing sandalfoot pantyhose with reinforced crotches. What was her baby trying to tell Mumma, that away from home, Jane transformed into a teenaged sensual thrill-seeker with low impulse control, so she needed to reign herself in during Lent? Did Jane think Mumma acted too straightlaced, too uptight and the Lenten proposals acted as a futile prod for loosening Mumma's laces? Most likely, Mumma concluded, Jane entangled her mother in plain and simple divine punishment, not hellfire and damnation, heaven knows, but that steady, pesky annoyance delivered cheerfully by a child to humble the pluckiest parent.

When the proposals evolved to extreme sports a few years ago, she agreed with Jane to give up motocross, sailboat racing on ice, the Paris-Dakar Rally. Still and all, Mumma fervently wishes that she just didn't have to think about what fresh weirdness her Jane is going to come up with every year. Of course Mumma didn't talk to Jane about Chinese New Year this year,

wanting to avoid all talk with Jane about observances and rituals so close to Lent. Why go making trouble for yourself?
Mumma didn't want to trigger the annual potentially sacrile-
gious Lenten chit-chat that Jane so eagerly posted on Mumma's
mental refrigerator.

....

Jane spends the two weeks before Lent, practising different
things to give up. This year, the one that's stuck so far: giving
up reading in bed. She loves kidding around with her mom,
but the discipline of actually giving up some bad habit makes
Jane feel religious, a compliance with a larger plan. Jane never
talks to Mumma about actual Lent observances. She read once
that it takes seventeen days to establish a new habit and extinguish an old one, and if, in the process, a person can become,
well, closer to, or part of, sort of, uhmm Devout, this has to be
a blessing, whatever blessing actually means.

Jane's embarrassed, too embarrassed to admit to anyone
that she determines reading in bed one of her worst vices. But
Chinese New Year's Eve, she sits on the toilet reading the weekend Religion section of the newspaper, this has been Jane's
practice every night for the past six, sitting on the toilet for
forty-five minutes, reading. [Note: a pelvic floor physiotherapist
will advise that you will pay dearly for reading while sitting
on the toilet, one of the worst habits you can adopt, a gigan-
tic down payment on anatomical systems complications in
your senior years, so what kind of risk are you willing to run?
Depends on you.]

"Aren't you coming to bed, yet?" Jane's husband calls. Leo
doesn't plan to give up anything for Lent.

Jane rereads the column in the Religion section of the newspaper, reporting that a group of forty Christians planned to spend the forty days of Lent in the Arizona desert on a prayer retreat, eating very spare, albeit daily catered meals, drinking only bottled water, and sleeping on camp cots set up in white canvas tents, to come to a more evolved understanding of Christian discipline and obedience. She folds the paper, runs her right thumb and index finger along the crease to sharpen it, and lays the paper on the bathroom tiles in front of her. The earnestness of the group's spokesperson as the article went on about atonement and self-denial has settled a leaden weight on Jane's chest bone. She can't quite dismiss the article as a bunch of people wanting to get away from it all but taking all the conveniences with them. Jane rests her elbows on her knees, her jaw cradled by the heels of two fists.

That she didn't get Lent straight comes as no surprise to Jane. She's shaky on all religious concepts and observances. She's tried to shed light on her spiritual muddle, [Note: Yes, a generous share of Mumma's muddle got scooped out of the pool of wiggly bits and spiral chains, and poured into the DNA-and-mystery bucket that came to be known as Jane.] tried churches, temples, books, TED talks. She hoped for more than tepid and inconsistent results. She thinks about "playing church" at home when they were children, none of the Lee kids understanding very much of what went on in church, Tom breaking open a giant loaf of unsliced sandwich bread, and Jane pouring Welch's grape juice into a cup. When bread was no longer delivered to the house, Dad brought warm egg loaf bread home from Alberta Bakery. He placed the loaves on the kitchen table, and when he opened the bags so the bread could cool, she and

Tom would sneak one slice, cut it carefully into little squares of bread, and put the squares on Mumma's glass tea plate. Then they would take turns serving each other, with one walking solemnly, holding the plate in two hands and standing in front of the other who would receive communion, sitting properly on a tiny child's folding chair, and taking only one small square of bread. In the hundreds of versions of make-believe they played together over the years, playing church was the only one that didn't end in a fight and tears.

And yet, Jane realizes, she and Tom together in real life church never could be anything but miserable and combative with each other, Tom frowning as Jane drained the last half of the tiny glass communion cup that Dad handed to her after all the adults but no children were invited to drink.

Jane thinks of the last time she visited Mumma and Dad on her own, and they went to church. Sunday last Fall, no communion, and after a brief, still incomprehensible service for Jane, the congregation went downstairs for lunch. Here it comes, Jane thought, everyone talking Chinese to me, and Mumma still bailing me out.

A few of the men in the congregation, many of them retired cooks from the best restaurants in the city, had prepared a No Particular Reason feast in the basement of the church, where there was a kitchen and a hall. Turkey with sticky rice dressing plump with chopped up sausage, Chinese mushrooms, scallions, and shrimp; cellophane noodles with eight different vegetables; braised beef hotpot with tofu, onions and Chinese melon; steamed pork buns; roasted chicken with salt crispy skin; barbeque duck from the barbeque place; Chinese broccoli, guy lan, wok-fried then steamed in a ginger garlic broth;

deep-fried rock cod topped by a hot and tangy-sweet sauce; round carrot coins carved into rabbit and flower shapes, with green beans, sweet onion, and button mushrooms. All these dishes timed to be ready right at the end of the service, and set up along a series of rectangular tables, large rectangular metal pans fit into an endless line of steaming trays.

"Happy Sunday, Moi Moi!" [Note: Moi Moi means little sister in Cantonese.] Uncle Kenny said, as he handed Jane a large, clean stainless steel cooking spoon, "You on guy lan, Numbah 5 steamah. Go!" Uncle Kenny was a cook in Maple Creek, Saskatchewan before he retired to Edmonton to live closer to his daughter.

No discussion, no, "I'm sorry I don't speak Chinese," no, I don't know how to do that, no need for Mumma to make three-decade-old excuses for Jane not talking to people. Suddenly, Jane stood on the serving line, dishing up Chinese broccoli to a stream of hungry people, holding their plates in front of her. Just dishing up greens, no language barrier, only smiling and serving and nodding, then dishing up the next scoop of guy lan. For the quickest moment, she bent forward and looked down the line of steamer trays at all the cooks and all the women who were also wielding steel spoons like hers. Jane felt a sense of kinship and belonging that she had never felt before. One of the cooks came behind her and replaced her almost empty pan, a fresh hot pan of guy lan slipped into the rim of the steamer tray. "C'mon, Moi Moi, people are hungry," he said.

Jane looks at the newspaper on the floor of her bathroom. She had forgotten all about how much fun she had dishing up lunch that day, the surprising feeling of lightness and belonging, the delicious food. She stands up, legs all crampy and wobbly, feels the welt of the vivid red ring around rosie, pulls down her night shirt, and goes to bed.

....

"**Good Morning, Mumma!** Happy New Year!" says Jane, the next morning, cradling the phone's receiver between her ear and her shoulder, as she packs her briefcase.

"Happy New Year to you too!"

"I'm just running out the door. But I wanted you to know what I've decided we should give up for Lent," Jane says, as she plucks the receiver out from under her jawbone.

Uh oh, thinks Mumma.

"Mumma, I think what we should give up for Lent this year, Ta-da: all this talk about what we're going to give up for Lent. We should just stop, not just for this year, but just stop. You do whatever you want about Lent, or not, and I'll do whatever I'm going to do — or not. But this year anyway, I'm not giving up anything, and we're not going to talk about Lent anymore. What do you think, Mumma?"

"Oh wow," Mumma says, "Oh wow."

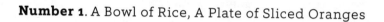

Number 1. A Bowl of Rice, A Plate of Sliced Oranges

They're all a little jumpy, sitting in the fin-tailed maroon Pontiac, travelling that day to see God. They have never been on such a long car ride. This is not the annual summer trip through Calgary to visit Li-Ting, Banff, Jasper, then home again. It will take most of the day just to get there. Dad in the driver's seat, twisting the fingers of his burgundy leather gloves. On the weekends, the gloves double as gardening gloves, the smell of peat moss and cut grass introducing themselves, how do you do, to the new car smell. Mumma, the navigator, fumbles with a road map, and finds home, Edmonton. What exactly a navigator does, Mumma can't say for sure. But, stove's turned off, iron's unplugged, fridge is empty. Garbage definitely out. One of the neighbours at the Old House forgot the garbage once. Chicken guts wrapped in brown paper, an orgy of putrefaction undulating under the kitchen sink while Morris and Nellie Brewin fed chipmunks along the Banff-Jasper parkway. Good old Morris, seized by uncontrollable urges for difficult meals, like homemade fried chicken, just before leaving on vacation. They bleached, they retiled, they repainted that whole kitchen, "bloody floor to ceiling," as Morris said, his nostrils flaring hairy caves, and still didn't get the smell out. Mumma pities Nellie at night, Morrie's red porous nose and those difficult-meal-hungry eyes between dear Nellie and the ceiling. Mumma will never forget to throw out the garbage, and to make sure, she has been throwing out little practice garbages every day for the past week.

Mumma pictures the suitcases in the trunk. One for her clothes and Dad's, his blue worsted with the vest taking up more than half the space, and one for the four kids. Each person has a dressy outfit, a cold weather outfit, shorts, two tee shirts, and a swimsuit. Mumma has packed a jar of soap flakes to rinse things out each night. Also a food box, a B.C. Apples cardboard flat, filled with cans of vegetable and chicken noodle soup, a loaf of bread, a jar of peanut butter and one of grape jelly, two tins of salmon, a sharp knife, and a can opener, just in case they have kitchenettes in the motels nearby to where God lives.

Last night, as Mumma pictured her husband and four children unclothed, tried to imagine what each one would need head to toe, skin to overcoat, Dad fiddled with the zipper pulls on the empty suitcases. "If the kids wear their dressy outfits, Mumma, I think we would only need one suitcase." The silvery lines feathering Mumma's lower abdomen dug in, as she folded three pairs of corduroy pants, brown, navy, and navy.

That man. If it were up to Dad, the kids would all drink a quart of orange juice, each, just before getting into the car, so no one would get thirsty and they wouldn't need to stop all day long, forget about toilet breaks.

"If the kids wear their dressy outfits, they will be all wrinkly and damp by the time we get there. They would get way too warm. Besides, you're forgetting something" — Mumma stuck her tongue out of her mouth, a baleful expression twisting her face.

Mumma turns around to review the troops, the four kids in the back seat. The youngest sits with her feet on the hump in the middle, both knees sporting a flesh-coloured bandage, not really flesh-coloured. Mumma studies each face slowly, particularly the eyes and the jawline, turning her head up and down as if to bring the picture into focus. The kids sit silently, take turns glaring at each other suspiciously.

"You," she points to the second youngest, Tom, "in the front seat." Tom stands up, and with one leg over the front seat, rolls over the top.

"I don't feel so good," he whimpers.

Dad rubs grey sneaker dust off his right shoulder, and turns the key in the ignition. A burgundy-gloved hand reaches behind the steering wheel to the gear shift lever, as Dad's driving oxford steps on the brake. He looks in the side view mirror down the long driveway, and then behind him to the three children in the back seat. Dad thinks, This is a good decision, taking the family to see God. "Ready?"

....

"You know, we could go to Saskatchewan this summer, ask your second cousin to be a translator when he's home visiting, reacquaint you with your extended family so they could tell you their stories."

"By car."

"Well, we'd have to have a car anyway. Why not? Great way to see the country."

"No thanks. I've had my share."

"Of what?"

"Car holidays. Country. Every year, Calgary for three days, Banff for two, Jasper for two, a day at home, then Dad would go back to work. Year after year, the six of us. We'd even stay in the same places. Number 6F, Chickadee Bungalows in Banff. Number 003, Whispering Pine Cabins, Jasper. In Calgary, we'd stay with Auntie Li-Ting when she still lived in her house. The house that smelled like dried shrimps and sweet rice steamed in bamboo leaves, the house where the rule was Don't Touch Anything, not that you would, nothing very interesting. Throughout the trip, we kids would take turns getting sick."

"Well, a car holiday wouldn't be like that now."

"Someone would start and for the rest of the week, each one of us, but no one more than once. Usually."

"I can imagine."

"No. You can't. You really can't."

"Same places. Every year?"

"Pretty well. And definitely, you could count on it being awful. Every year."

....

Mumma looks back at the house through the rear window. Cary Grant gently says to her, Oh Mumma, you looked back, then solemnly raises his hand slowly to say Goodbye. Vertical wooden siding wraps tightly around the bungalow, looks a paler shade of yellow in the shadow before sunrise. Grey striped canvas awnings shroud the square bedroom windows. The heads of three children form an uneven black, scalloped border on the picture Mumma develops for her memory album.

They haven't left the city, but nothing looks familiar, the east side of Edmonton a foreign country. Six heads swivel to observe the cement plant, the red brick Coca-Cola factory, the different but same Safeway store, the Beverly dump. "Traffic circle, Groat Road, 118th Avenue, Highway 16," Dad chants under his breath. Tom hugs his elbows and recites the numbers on the radio. Mumma's throat catches when farmers' fields appear in the windshield. This must mean they've driven out beyond the circle with the black star inside which marks Edmonton. The flatness initially fills her with a dread of falling off an edge, but the land's so unrelentingly flat, Mumma soon realizes the edge, if it comes, will be visible miles before they get there, and even Dad will be able to stop in time.

"Do we still go east, Mumma? We're coming to a junction. Again. Do we turn?"

She has enough on her mind, watching Tom turn progressively gill-ier, those creepy little "urps" shaking his round shoulders up and down. No one says anything, but everyone in the car is waiting for the same thing, like the start of a parade.

Mumma cracks open the map, looks for the circled dot called Calgary, their usual first stop on the annual trip, the customary trip with a familiar route and itinerary. Fools, that's what we are, she thinks. Fools. Dad, for this crazy notion, and me for going along with it.

"No, just keep going." Mumma folds the map back, wonders if this is what's expected of a navigator, if this is all she has to do.

Mumma turns her eyes to seven o'clock at Tom, whose eyelids are half shut. Maybe he'll nod off and they'll arrive without incident at the border, crossing the map from celery green Alberta to pale yellow Saskatchewan. Mumma wonders, Will the border be visible, miles ahead, fields shorn close in an alternating pattern of dots and dashes? Hmmm. She now regrets not listening when Dad had the map out on the kitchen table, every night for the past four, planning their trip. He said she'd have to be his navigator, that this was new territory for them. Then he talked about legends, touching the map with the tip of a wooden ruler. Writing numbers on a piece of paper, which he gave to Mumma, which she threw away by mistake in a practice garbage.

Mumma fidgets in her seat, the kids in the back seat too quiet. The girls distinctly noiseless since the car pulled out of the driveway before sunrise. They sit in a row as if they were in church, no, at the table after dinner, listening to their parents talk in Chinese. Alertness skips about their eyes. Out of the corners, six widening irises watch Dad's driving gloves gripping the wheel. The breeze coming in through Dad's little triangular window blows his hair in brilliantined strands of hot black tar.

"Stop. Pull over, stop the car, Dad," Mumma hollers, Tom's head jutting back and forth like a chicken. The gloves squeeze tighter on the steering wheel. Three heads in the backseat pull back slightly, become rigid atop their scrawny necks as Dad frowns in the rear view mirror. He checks his side mirror, the rear view mirror again, then shoulder checks wildly, as if he has blind spots crammed into every inch of glass. Mumma fumbles in her tote bag for an empty paper bag, as Dad methodically raises the signal arm with his left hand, then veers onto the shoulder. The soles of Mumma's sandals skid on the gravel as she pulls on Tom's arm. They just make it away from the back of the car. Lucky, this time.

....

"Gosh, that throwing up, it must have been like Agatha Christie's, *And Then There Were None*. Someone was going to be next, but who?"

"Ho-ho, what a funny man. It wasn't so much the sick, as the tension. Sitting in the middle, over the hump, I remember Mumma, keeping an eye on the one most likely to, but, still pretending like this was the best time ever, she would turn to the rest of us. With the windows open, her permy curls would shoot out in front of her forehead, her voice seemed to broadcast, disembodied, from the thickest, wiry curl: 'We're almost there.' And then she'd smile. We knew she had no idea where there was. She had no idea where here was. She would fold and unfold maps, Avon lady smile painted on her face, and we squirmed.

"Which was much easier than thinking, even for one moment, about Dad, the scary driver. There's something about the long blare of another car's horn when you're travelling at highway speed that you never forget. Just thinking about it makes me feel nauseated, like the grim reaper's scythe casually nicking the back of my shirt. On occasion, we pitched from side to side, a boat in a storm. And forty minutes after he finished driving for the day, Dad's hands still curled like they were gripping the steering wheel. Scary driver, we kids knew what the finger meant before anyone told us."

"Your Dad wasn't driving any more by the time I met you. But he had such a small stature, I can't imagine he would have had a very easy time of it, driving those big old American cars."

"Well, Dad got a lot smaller by the time you met him. He learned to drive from the salesman who sold him his first car. Four circuits around the lot, Dad in the driver's seat, as the salesman sat with his arm over the front seat, pointing out the controls. In those days, after the war, getting your driver's license was a matter of paying a fee, no practical test, no test for whether you understood the rules of the road. He did, but still. And never had an accident, but still."

"Good grief, Charlie Brown. But seriously, I think we should go to Saskatchewan. Those stories mean so much to you. I'd love to see the land, the country. And this time, for you, with air conditioning."

"Right. See the country. What a great idea, from the man who's never been on a real road trip. Gas station johns, seedy motels. You'd be disappointed. Worse, I'll be disappointed: what if a road trip meets, or, even worse, exceeds your expectations? I would lose all respect for you, clucking and cooing over those motel bathroom condiments."

"Like?"

"Tiny, stinky, little soaps wrapped in cheap shiny paper. Waxy paper ice buckets printed with a faux wood pattern. Plastic cups wrapped in plastic film. You know, no hair dryers, no white terry bathrobe, no room service, no mini-bar fridge. They're very old, some of the motels, extremely retro. What if you like all that stuff, what if you go all gaga over motel road trips? Maybe they'll be like a Pandora's Tacky Sister's Box that I'll have wished you kept shut."

"Let's leave tomorrow."

....

The time had come to take the children to see God. Now, right this moment. All enrolled in school and doing well, and only Pen seemed in the middle of an awkward period, all gangly, her face growing faster than her hair, her sulkiness growing faster still. The time seemed right, to Dad. And even though Dad didn't enjoy driving, especially dreaded driving away from home on roads he had never driven on, the way the kids were growing, the family would never line up, height-wise, quite so nicely as they did right now. Dad, Mumma, Lizzie, all the way down to the baby, a perfect wedge from Dad right down to the ground. He wanted to present that image to God, the family starting firmly at ground level ascending and ending with Dad. Rehearsing this scene in his mind, over and over, Dad's quiet face would scream at God, "Ha. Take that."

"Mumma, what's 'twnshp'? If we stay on this road, we miss 'twnshp'. Sounds important. Maybe you should look at the map." Dad turns his head toward Mumma as a green sedan careens past, the sound wave of its horn flaring and fading in the open car windows. Even with wind funnelling through the open windows, a close, milky odour permeates the car interior. Tom sits in the back seat behind Mumma's head, his eyes closed. Pen flops her head back and forth between Mumma and Dad. Dad, afraid his voice will be muted by the wind, feels himself screaming. His left eye winces at the air pressure. With Mumma guiding the way, Dad takes comfort that they will see God in no time. He thinks that Mumma's birthplace, Calgary, makes her a natural at figuring out the roads, the country. His upper lip peels skyward in the wind, showing more pink gum than he intends. During a flop to her left, Pen thinks she's seen bits of what Dad's head would look like as a skeleton. She buries her head into the car seat under Mumma's shoulder.

"Can I see the map?" Lizzie asks from the back seat.

"No," Dad replies, "Mumma's the navigator. What about 'twn-shp', Mumma? Can you find it on the map? Mumma?"

"Keep going, Dad," Mumma says, taking stock of the three heads in the back seat, the breath under her arm feeling kitten warm.

.... ,

"Those stories about your Dad's family. They're so puzzling. I don't get them. Makes you want more, doesn't it? Doesn't it make you want more? What about those people in Saskatchewan?"

"Two problems with what you're suggesting. First, they don't speak any English. Really at all. And you know me. When the talking starts, I'm completely at sea. I know House of the Lord, and dim sum, but that spreads thin, fast."

"What about your second cousin? We could time our trip there when he goes to visit next, he could be your translator."

"Donny? Are you kidding? He barely understands now. Says he lost the tongue, then the understanding, he can't even carry on a conversation with his mother anymore."

"I don't think it's that simple to lose a language."

"Hard, you mean hard, it's not that hard. And, anyway, I think what you're suggesting is predatory. I can't presume to visit someone just so they will tell me stories."

"Predatory, you mean, to claim your family history."

"Claim? Claim. Wow. And what makes you think people want to talk about the past?"

"There, you are wrong. My Scottish Grammy, she used to love telling us stories of life on the prairies. All you had to say to her was, 'Grammy, what was it like when you pulled water up from the ground in a bucket' and she'd be off. Marvelous."

"Not everyone has perky, upbeat stories. What if they're hurtful stories, and I come along saying, 'Would you mind picking the scab off that please, because that's my family history and I'm here to Claim it.' Those relatives in Saskatchewan, they aren't plucky prairie people. They aren't chafing at the bit to tell plucky prairie stories."

"Of course. But —"

"Buggy whips and corsets. Buckboard wagons. And linen trousseaus. Won't find that stuff in my family's inventory. Maybe your family history, but not mine."

....

Mumma zips open the kids' suitcase, the edge of the car trunk resting on the top of her head. Pen stands behind the car in her Ladybug Underwear undershirt, her hands balled into the cups of her armpits. Mumma rifles through, pulls out a striped tee shirt, hands it to Pen, and tucks another paper bag package into the hole of the spare tire. Raising her right hand to the lip of the trunk, Mumma discovers her head actually feels better supporting the trunk's weight. She pulls a roll of foil wrapped mints out of her housedress pocket and hands them to her daughter. Pen thanks Mumma quietly, ducks under the clean tee shirt. Holding the trunk lid high with one hand, Mumma raises one leg flamingo to flick out the gravel underneath the heel of her sandal.

Well, we've barfed in Saskatchewan, Mumma thinks, feeling sassy using the word, barf, albeit only in her mind and to herself. On Saskatchewan, barfed on Saskatchewan, she thinks. There was no warning, no sign they would imminently cross the border. All of a sudden, bang, Welcome to Saskatchewan. Then all of a sudden, bang, up on the gravel shoulder again.

Mumma rubs her neck with her free hand, and recollects Dad's stories. When Dad came to southern Saskatchewan with his father and all the uncles, they landed in a pile of misfortune: post-war uncertainty when national war departments at home and abroad weren't buying any more grain to feed troops; a regional drought dried out a land that barely sustained the scraps of life already there; and a community memory still lingered of beloved young men, their own kin, coming home from the Great War and infecting townsfolk with Spanish Flu, suddenly killing hundreds of children and young adults in the area (a newspaper from the capital saying thousands dead across the province), fear shutting doors firmly on friends, on neighbours. Arriving as outsiders, aliens to this landscape of adversity, how would they survive, let alone thrive, when even the smallest blade of grass seemed to say No. Mumma remembers what Dad says: They landed in a time of misfortune so bad, the uncles stayed put. Just stayed put, for generations. Waiting for hairline cracks to plant roots that might not exist just to endure hardship, but to flourish.

The plan didn't work for all of them. Dad's father left Canada after a few years, returning to the home that was no longer home, to a wife no longer living. "She died of a broken heart," Dad's father told him, when the letter containing the news of her broken heart finally arrived. "She died of a broken heart," Dad told Mumma, unsolicited, before she was Mumma, before he was Dad, when they were still their own names. "She died of a broken heart," Mumma told Tom last Thanksgiving, when Teacher asked about his missing grandparents in the drawing of his family tree.

Mumma lowers but does not close the trunk lid and gives the long road in front of the car a once-over. Dad has brought them far too close to the edge, and Mumma might not manage to haul them back in time. More than ever, Mumma yearns for the instincts of a navigator, although she's still uncertain what, exactly, that means.

Something, an absence, catches Mumma's attention, as she flings the car trunk skyward. Eyes scan two suitcases, food box, extra paper bags. Shoe box. Shoe box? Shoe box.

The baby has gone down to the floor on one side of the back seat, and lies down with her head resting on the hump. The remaining three sit in the back seat, the hump separating them: one yet to blow and two already done.

"We've forgotten the shoe box, Dad," Mumma says, closing the front passenger door behind her.

"What's that?"

"The shoe box. All the kids' shoes, and your dress shoes. And mine. All the shoes."

"We can't go back."

"I know. I thought you should know." Mumma wishes she had the verve, the nerve to say, Let's call the whole thing off, Dad. Big Sign, forgetting that shoe box. She puckers her lips to one side.

Dad turns his head, "You mean the kids will be wearing rubber thongs when we get there? Dressy clothes and rubber thongs?"

"Or sneakers," Mumma says, "whatever they have on their feet. Me too, and you too. I think we better stop, have lunch and something to drink. These kids look ready for a break."

"We'll stop at the next café. Maybe we can find a place to buy shoes."

Mumma's no longer sure Dad will be able to stop in time. Dad signals off the shoulder, readjusting the image in his mind of what he has to show to God. In the rear view mirror, the chrome grill of a red sports car looms like shark's teeth. Dad's mind processes the shark teeth as he passes an orange sign: "Road Construction Ahead."

....

"That story your second cousin Don told us tonight, do you think that's true?"

"What, about my grandmother?"

"Yeah, isn't that wild, your Grammy is, like, village folklore. She was, you know, a cautionary tale. Just because she forgot and threw out 'the stem or the end' of the spring tonic bean. A bad reaction, and she didn't have the antidote."

"You find this entertaining? An amusement, a party piece?"

"No. It just seems so amazing, unreal, in light of that 'died of a broken heart' story you told me when we first started seeing each other. Do you think your father even knew this story?"

"I don't know. Whenever I asked him, all he ever said was, 'she died of a broken heart'. That's all I know, I think that's all he knew. He refused to go back to visit. Of course, he only had a sister left by then, and she didn't even live in the village anymore. Dad used to get these letters in the '60s from the Chinese government saying that his sister was unwell, needed money. Letters that didn't even have the decency to stop coming after he heard she had died. I don't know what he knew. And I don't know what the real story is. Donny's mother lived there at the time, but she was so young, just a girl. I don't know."

"So don't you want to find out? Don't you want to know what happened?"

....

In town, the baby looks up over the café at the painted sign of a tawny beige peanut and decides this is a splendid place to vomit. Still getting accustomed to her family calling her Jane some of the time, and not always "the baby" (Jane, the name her teacher and the other kids called her at playschool this past year), Jane feels like she's woken up from her nap on Mumma and Dad's bed, the white chenille bedspread impressing a waffle weave pattern on her hot, sticky face. But her tummy's a queasy whirlpool and Jane's old enough to know and say that Tummy needs a place to backtrack, and fast. No longer an infant, but still small enough, Mumma plucks the baby off the car floor and runs with her, football-style, through the centre aisle of the restaurant to the washroom at the back. One vacant cubicle makes a passable end zone for Mumma and Jane, touchdown. [Note: Mumma will remember always that Jane measured thirty-six inches, and thirty-six pounds when she started Grade 1 that September, smaller than her other children but not significantly so. The newly-graduated school nurse will call Mumma at home, asks her why Jane is so small; does Mumma have enough food available to give to

223

Jane at mealtimes; does Mumma know about the Canada Food Guide. Since Jane's not that much smaller than her siblings at the same age, and the school nurse never called home about the older kids, Mumma will give the young nurse an intense practical education that the new graduate's university failed to provide. Mumma will have enough pieces of her mind left to pack back into her <59-inch frame which will prove conducive to recalling, for the rest of her life, her pissed-off fury at the school nurse who dared to question Mumma's ability to Mumma just because she had compact kids. For her part, the school nurse will never forget how dangerous it is to walk between a cub and a Mumma bear.]

Dad kneels beside the car, his fingers running along the laches of warm, oily tar, especially thick by the front wheel wells, then feathering out, flanking both sides of the beautiful maroon car, a monster woman's false eyelashes. The three children stand beside Dad. He stops inspecting the tar and turns to the kids' feet. Rubber thongs that come between the first and second toe, seem to stretch the toe bones into long overreaching digits. Grey white sneakers with a hole in the toe, and small, red canvas slip-ons with Augie Doggie on the vamp, one stained a dark blotchy red.

Dad stands up and rubs his hands on the fronts of his pants. No shoe stores on this street, but if they watch very carefully where they eat, there should be enough money for three pairs of new shoes. Dad looks up at the peanut sign over the café, and motions the children inside.

He can't spot Mumma anywhere, but the proprietor comes to the front of the restaurant, greets Dad enthusiastically, and begins to speak. Acknowledging each other with eye movements and barely a head turn, the three kids stand silently as the words volley back and forth over their heads. The proprietor takes them to a booth with green vinyl seats, as Mumma appears from the ladies' room with the baby in tow, wiping her hands across the front of her tee shirt. Mumma and Dad sit near the wall on either side, settling the controversy over who gets to sit by the little wall-mounted jukebox. [Note: Mumma and Dad will always sit on the outside seats of a booth after today, even after tableside jukeboxes disappear.] The children slowly fall in line into the booth seats.

At an adjacent table, three men in dark work pants and long leather jackets drink coffee. They talk amongst themselves, and one of them smiles at Tom, who sits on the end, kicking his feet in the air.

"Hey kid. You on summer vacation?"

"Yeah." Mumma's head snaps in Tom's direction. She centres her attention on Tom, her menu frozen in mid-air. Dad notices Mumma and turns casually in the direction of the men's table.

"Where you going?" the man asks.

"I don't know," Tom replies, not looking at him.

"Well that's real nice. You here for lunch, then?"

"Mm hmm," Tom says.

"What's your favourite, kid? What do you like to eat best?"

Tom wants to be a gentleman, knows he should make eye contact with the man like Dad taught him, but Tom can't make himself. Instead, he slowly turns his head sideways, "I don't know. I guess steak and potatoes."

The man's jaw opens wide, as if wired on a flat hinge. His laugh comes out of the hole at the back of his mouth in rough, breathy gasps.

"Leave the kid alone, Clem."

"No. That's great. I think that's great. Who taught you to say that, kid? That's great," Clem says, between breaths.

Mumma feels her throat constricting against the bottom of her jaw. Dad smiles at the men, and says, "That's my boy. Yeah. That's my son. They're all my children," he says.

"Well there sure are enough of them mister," Clem replies.

"Yes," Dad says quickly, "and all of them good. Nice to spend some time with my family. We're on vacation. Drove through some tar back on the highway. Any of you fellows know what takes tar off a car?"

Dad notices the men being gentlemen to each other, lots of eye contact. Expressionless.

"Sorry," Clem says, not looking at Dad, "Don't know."

"Well nice talking to you," Dad says, tipping his forefinger off the brim of an imaginary hat.

"Watch out for goofs on the road," Clem says to no one in particular, as he moves his coffee cup to his mouth, "Too many goofs on the road these days. Goofs and kooks."

When the hamburgers arrive, Mumma takes the pickles and tomato out of the bun and nibbles on them until the men vacate the adjacent table.

After lunch, the kids rotate through the bathroom. Dad goes to talk to the proprietor standing by the cashier who refuses to take Dad's money. Dad presses some bills into the palm of the proprietor, who follows Dad out, showering the family with a blizzard of dialogue.

....

"It wasn't really a case of food poisoning. More of a home poisoning? I don't know. Would you call that spring tonic, food? Which food group?"

"You're not stuck on this still, are you?"

"Well, yes. I am. We wouldn't have to drive there. I can understand, that association. We can fly into, I guess, Regina or Saskatoon, and get a u-drive."

"You sound more interested in pursuing my family history than I do. You want to seek out my roots, my bamboo shoots? It's not just the driving."

"I'm interested because of you. I want you to have this. I want you to know your father better. You were his baby, and you were so close, but you didn't really know him."

"Stop."

"But this way, you can keep getting to know him, get closer. It's the only way."

"Don't you think I have enough? I can barely handle what I do know. Do I want to know more about an eight-year-old-boy, the English words learned first, in school, a parochial school oh God is great, his first English words in the world, 'heathen Chinee'. What more is there to know? Names can hurt like sticks and stones, and memories can break your bones. Don't know that version, do you?"

"You only see the worst. You need the whole story."

"'Tell me your whole story, but leave out the bad parts.' Is that what I should say? 'Tell me your story, but watch out for my heart. It's a family weakness.' You go too far."

"You don't push yourself hard enough."

"You standing there, telling me where to draw the line. Telling me I need the whole story, when you don't even know what that story might be. That's rich. Go discover your own roots, Mr. Columbus. I've been to Saskatchewan before, you know."

....

"**Well, there isn't a shoe store anyway.**" Dad realizes that, with lunch, and with the time change, they have lost the beginning of the heat of the day, great, but precious time, as well. "People buy their shoes by catalogue here. Draw their feet onto cardboards and hope for the best." Dad shakes his head.

They sit in the car, the windows down, the baby drifting off to sleep in the front seat. Mumma's lids feel heavy too, the children usually not ill in such rapid succession. Dad turns the ignition key and slowly moves the car away from the curb.

"How many more miles from here, Mumma? I don't remember."

Mumma runs the fingertip of her ring finger along her eyebrow. "Let me look at the map." Mumma spreads open the road map of Saskatchewan and pretends to study, the costume of the navigator weighing heavily upon her.

"Where are we?" Mumma asks.

"What do you mean? Battleford, we're in North Battleford, and right up ahead, there's the highway. Going to White Rose through Saskatoon."

"We'll get there, Dad."

"I know that, but when? How far?" Dad eases back onto the highway, and turns his head towards Mumma, his eyebrows arching in the middle of his forehead like a temple roof.

"Well. Let's see. This far." Mumma moves her hand from the map, and raises her fingers in front of Dad's face, her thumb and forefinger spanning an invisible line of about four inches.

"How far?"

"Like this, Dad."

Gravel pops like machine gun fire as Dad pulls onto the shoulder. "What do you mean, like this?" he says, mimicking Mumma's hand gesture.

"That's how far it is to White Rose. That's what the map says."

"Oh," Dad says, his icy calm blanketing the car. Dad floors the gas pedal, obscuring the back windshield with dust. As suddenly, he brakes, sending five bodies forward and plastering them back into their seats. "That far, Mumma?"

"I quit," Mumma declares. "We never should have come here. If it's so important for you to read this country," she says, throwing the map into Dad's lap, "Go right ahead."

The kids have an image in the rear view mirror of Dad's eyes growing wider and wider as he studies the map.

"We'll never make it," he says, in disbelief, "We will never make it. It's too far."

Mumma rolls her eyes. "Then just call the man. Tell him we got delayed. Tell him we won't make it until tomorrow."

Call God, Dad thinks. Ring God up, and tell him we're running a little late. Tell God to please wait on his sickly family, with the tarry car, and the throw-up runners. No bloody way. We may be many things to God, things that he's wrong about, but we are not going to be late.

Dad turns off the car and pockets the keys in his hand. He opens his door and walks toward the back of the car. Five heads follow his progress, Where will he will stop? He opens the trunk and removes the two suitcases. He hands one suitcase into the back, the other one to Mumma.

"We'll change on the way. Everyone, we're going to see Him."

....

"This Father Brady, he was held up to us by Dad when we were young as a definitive moral yardstick. 'What would Father Brady say?' 'Father Brady wouldn't be pleased to hear you did that.' On and on. The principal of the only school in the area, and that's who taught Dad how to speak English. Your principal is your pal, some bloody spelling lesson. My dad left school in Canada after completing only one year. That's why all of us wallowed in university so long. Still, Dad was so much brighter, more intelligent than all of us put together, and just so determined. I don't know what happened, why he left school. He always said he had to help his father and uncles in the restaurant, but now everything he told me, I wonder. It wasn't until I was older that I knew more of that Father Brady story, that heathen Chinee business. Wicked old fart."

....

No, not really, not a flash before your eyes, Mumma thinks. She concentrated on whether or not her neighbours, Eileen and Sally, and her sister Moe would have thought any differently of her, going through her house afterwards. She had washed the floors, but if she had it all to do over again, she definitely would have found the time to clean the oven. Mumma's legs bend jointless as she leans on the side of the car, retching beside the front tire.

Dad has ducked behind a tree to change into his blue worsted, with the vest. Lizzie has pulled a turquoise rat-tail comb out of her purse and combs all the other kids' hair. They stand in a row, as Dad demanded. Fresh from flying over several swells in the asphalt, the kids all have flushed cheeks. They try to give Dad some privacy, but their attention keeps going back to the tree. The kids assess the school grounds where God lives to be pretty average.

Dad emerges from behind the tree, running a comb quickly through his hair. When he sees Mumma wiping her mouth with a Kleenex, Dad decides not to insist that she change into her blue dress with the matching cropped jacket.

He sits in an office sucking a wet stubby end of a cigar that even the baby notices has gone out, long extinguished. Pink capillaries network across the bulbs over his nostrils. On His walls, a gallery of engraved wooden plaques surrounds Him like mosaic tiles. He invites Mumma to sit in the only other chair in the room, and nestles his buttocks further down into the chair behind his desk. Dwarfing him are haphazard mounds of paper on his desk and the floor. Most of the ash from his cigar rests in the crevasses of his black-panted lap.

He doesn't remember Dad.

"But I came to your school. Many years ago. You taught me."

"Been a lot of students through here you know." Father Brady speaks to the ascending heads standing in front of him. Dad can't help but wish Mumma stood beside him, to ensure their perfect, sloping wedge.

"But I was here. Nineteen twenty-one."

He pulls a book off a shelf behind Him, and leafs through its pages, slows at one section of the book and stops to read an entry. "Oh, by God. Yes, you were. That's you is it? Lee?"

The kids stare at Him. At him. He doesn't look anything like the legend they've heard about all their lives. [Note: There should be a word that means this: I didn't have a specific picture in my mind, but seeing you now and all the myriad details that culminate in you, all these aspects of you may come the closest to the dead-on picture of what I never could have imagined you would look like.] To start with, the kids never ever thought he could have ashy pants.

"And Lee, I presume Mrs. Lee and the family."

"We drove all day to see you. I wanted the children to meet you." Dad's so relieved that He doesn't stand up and see the children's shoes.

"Well, they're fine-looking children," Father Brady says, dropping his wet stub into a tarnished metal ashtray of stubs, "and the first thing you have to do, you must teach these children how to speak English."

Wing's shoulder blades fall back against the office wall as if he'd been pushed. Aghast, Wing Lee tries to translate Father Brady, His face, His...those words. Mumma raises herself up in her chair, feels the bones of her back stack up one on top of the other.

"These children. Our children speak perfect English," she says, standing up, asserting her gentlewomanly eye contact and extending her hand confidently. "A pleasure to finally meet you, face to face. Children, we will be leaving now, please say your goodbyes."

Without asking, the kids line up still in that perfect wedge from Jane, Tom, Pen and Lizzie. Dad's shoulder blades come off the wall to support his squared shoulders. He cups Mumma's elbow, as he stands beside her, watching his children shake hands with him, firmly and business-like, and don't forget eye contact like you really see the person, exactly as Dad has taught them all.

As they pull out of the parking lot, the kids giggle uncontrollably. "He was so dirty... Wow did you see those ashes on his lap... What a turkey... 'These children must learn how to speak English'." The voice is so well imitated, Dad laughs, and turning his head to the back seat, he wags his haha-naughty finger.

"Now you kids," Dad says into the rear-view mirror.

The fin-tailed maroon Pontiac turns onto the highway, in search of a clean unit with a kitchenette.

"Please, Dad? Can we find a motel with a swimming pool? An outdoor swimming pool?"

"Well sure. Let's look for one Mumma," he offers, gently grasping the hand of his navigator.

Author's Note

This is a work of fiction. Places, characters, names, and events described (or noted as something that would happen in the future) formed in my imagination, or are presented fictitiously — you can read more about that at the front of the book. And yes, there is such a thing as coincidence, where fictional stories about fictional people, places, and events resemble only by coincidence whatever we may conceive of as real, or actual, life.

I am not an expert in anything, so nothing in this book should be taken as professional advice. It is not the function or intention of this book to encourage or discourage anyone from seeking advice (including professional advice) on any subject. This book is fiction, makes no representations on the value of expert opinions, and should not be used to replace or interpret expert opinions. That all being said, in my humble opinion, there are better things you could do for yourself than sitting on the toilet to read. Consider a new place to love reading. Seriously.

The locations of some former places of business in my beloved home province of Alberta may not be geographically accurate, especially in relation to one another, and what a shame if municipal history aficionados are disappointed. Please bear in mind, I was a kid when I observed some of these places and I still have a sense of direction that could use a little improvement.

Finally, so there can be no misunderstanding, the fictional Lee family is not the family into which I was born. Mumma and Wing are not my parents, Moe and Li-Ting are not my aunts, Paul is not my cousin, Don is not my second cousin, and Jane, Lizzie, Pen, and Tom are not my siblings and myself. While the people in my birth family were and are all amazing characters in their own right, they are not the characters in these stories.

Acknowledgments

A previous version of "Number 88. Spicy Beef in Lettuce Wraps" appeared in *Boundless Alberta*, published by NeWest Press and edited by Aritha van Herk.

I want to thank the good people at NeWest Press who said Yes to this book, and those who worked so hard to bring the book to life. I acknowledge the amazing gift that saying Yes means to me, and will always mean to me. And in the process of publishing the book, for a while, Paul, then Matt and Claire at NeWest were unfailingly cheerful, easy to work with, optimistic, and fun, and made this adventure a true joy ride. Thank you.

The word has not been invented to properly express my gratitude for all the energy and focus, time, brilliance, encouragement and shelter that the editor of this book, Nicole Markotić, gave to this manuscript. Thank you, Nicole. If I know one thing that's true, it's this: this collection of stories finally grew up and left home to become a book because of Nicole.

Many years ago, I took writing classes in the English department at the University of Calgary for three years, and it was in that workshop environment, that I travelled with this ever-changing, talented community of people who were simultaneously discovering the joy and aardvark (hard work) of sitting quietly to craft a story. While we dispersed back to our lives, you are never far away in my mind, and neither are your characters nor your stories. Thank you. I will never stop hoping for the realization of your dreams.

No community thrives without exceptional leadership, and I acknowledge receiving the patient and profoundly gifted guidance, instruction, and inspiration from my teachers at U of C, Professor Aritha van Herk, and Professor Nicole Markotić, gifts that never end. Thank you.

Life has graced me with friends and family whose constancy, support, encouragement, and cooking have fed me over countless years. I am humbled by their kindness and love. However, rather than naming the generous, caring people who made me laugh, never gave up hope, and gently but firmly aligned my wheels — you know who you are, I know who you are, and I thank you very much.

And to my husband, Mike, who bears all things. This book could not have happened without you. Thank you.

Permissions

IT'S MY PARTY
Words and Music by HERB WIENER, JOHN GLUCK and WALLY GOLD
© 1963 (Renewed) CHAPPELL & CO., INC.
All Rights Reserved
Used by Permission of ALFRED MUSIC

You Call Everybody Darling
Words and Music by Sam Martin, Ben Trace and Clem Watts
(c) 1946 (Renewed) EDWIN H. MORRIS & COMPANY, A Division of MPL Music
Publishing, Inc.
All Rights Reserved
Reprinted by Permission of Hal Leonard Corporation

"I Enjoy Being a Girl"
Copyright © 1958 by Richard Rodgers and Oscar Hammerstein II
Copyright Renewed.
Williamson Music (ASCAP), an Imagem Company owner of publication and
allied rights throughout the World. All Rights Reserved.

¶ This book was set in Carat and Equip, both designed by Dieter Hofrichter at Hoftype.

Lauralyn Chow was born, raised, and educated in Edmonton, Alberta. Her first summer job was at a radio station and she later worked as the first in-house lawyer for the Calgary Board of Education (the public school board). She has a B.A. in Psychology, minoring in Sociology, and an LL.B. from the University of Alberta. When she visits Hawaii, which she does frequently, she is often mistaken for a local and once won an air ukulele contest during the Aloha Festivals. She currently resides in Calgary, Alberta.